Dear Addie

Gracie's
Garden

Happy Birthday

by
Jamie Mock

eimaj publishing
2010

For information regarding permission, write to eimaj publishing,
Attention: Permissions Department, P.O. Box 927 Murphy, NC 28906

ISBN-13 # 978-0-9844224-1-8

Printed in the U.S.A.
First paperback printing, February 2010

Release Date - March 20, 2010

About the Art & the Book

A special thank-you to Mark Menendez for
working with me to bring to life the characters and the covers
of the Gracie's Garden book series.

To illustrate pictures that lie within the imagination and
dreams of another is a difficult task. Fortunately, for Gracie's Garden,
Mark Menendez agreed to become the hand that moved the brush.

Often changing directions, that brush has brought forth a beautiful
place for children to visit and special friends to keep them company.
It's a safe place, a special place..... a place to learn and play.

Children need these places to develop the kind of character and
imagination that will guide them to triumph in their work of tomorrow.

Creativity, Intelligence, Positive Energy and Love:
What better friends for children to play with?

To bring these characteristics forward in their work of tomorrow,
is to give the children of tomorrow..... a better place.

Isn't that what it's all about?

Jamie Mock

For My Children

Madison
Zachary
Roanin
Bailey
&
Gracie

I am only the pen.
You are the ink.

Welcome

Welcome to Gracie's Garden.
Gracie's Garden is for everyone.
It's a special place..... a safe place,
  a place to learn and play.

Gracie is a little girl who loves to be outside.
She lives in the big white house on the hill.
The Garden was built by her father.
It was built for Gracie and all her friends.

YOU! are welcome to visit Gracie's Garden any time.
Day or night and all through the year,
 the gate is never locked.

Just follow the pretty, white picket fence.
It leads to the big, bright, white garden gate.
Open the door..... and step inside.
But don't forget to close the gate behind you.

Remember,
You are welcome anytime!
Even if Gracie isn't there.

Oh!
Before you go, let me tell you a few things
  about the Garden.

First..... Be careful.
  Walk on the garden path.
  Look where you are going.
  Gracie's plants and all her friends are little.
  You don't want to hurt them.

Second..... Enjoy yourself and have fun.
  Explore the Garden from beginning to end.
  If you don't understand something..... ask someone.

Finally..... Gracie is not there right now.
  But if you keep your eyes open, and look carefully,
   you might meet Gracie's very best friends!

Oh, there is just one more thing I need to tell you.

Recently, Gracie carried a little box into the Garden.
Inside, there was a very special snail.
Gracie put him in a small, safe place.
It's a hollow space between two rotting boards.
She named him Sammy.
He usually comes out at dark.

Sammy is a slimy little snail.
He is slow and slimy and somewhat stinky.
He is new to Gracie's Garden.

Sammy is a very special kind of snail.
He is a delicate Decollate snail.
        (Deck- Uh - Lit)
Decollate snails eat Garden Snail eggs.

Sammy is very important to Gracie and her garden.
        So, if you meet him, be nice to him.
                Gracie does not want him to leave.

IV

Chapter 1

Spring had arrived.
It had been a perfect day in the Orange Grove.
Sunny..... with a warm gentle breeze.
White blossoms decorated trees in the green valley.
And now the sun was settling down for the evening.
A deep orange glow twinkled through the branches.
Warm dewdrops fell to the ground.

The Decollate snails were already awake.
They were searching the soft damp soil,
  searching for hidden treasures.

Sammy's voice broke the evening's silence.
  "I found them! I found them!" he shouted.
He was so excited to be the first to find them.
His family and friends would be so proud.

The other Decollate snails rushed over.

"Incredible!" said his cousin Robbie.

"There are so many!" said his friend Keith.

"Every one of them looks perfect!" said his neighbor Bruce.

Everyone stared at the treasure in silence.
Little round pearls glowed in the last light of the day.

His father's deep, proud voice thundered,
  "Son, you have a gift! I don't know how you do it!
    These are the best Garden Snail eggs I have ever seen!"

This was the second time Sammy had found eggs this week.
Sammy beamed with satisfaction.

Suddenly, everything changed.
Bright lights came flashing.
Intense, blinding lights washed over them.
Sammy could hardly see what was happening.

Keith was grabbed from above. He disappeared.
Bruce slid for his life down into the nest of eggs.
Sammy turned around quickly. Robbie was gone.

The bright light in the night sky blinded him.
The outline of his father lifted up off the ground.
  "Slide and Hide!" he yelled down to Sammy.
Then his father was swallowed up by the flash of light,
  pulled up and away into the dark night sky.
Sammy was alone. His friends and family were gone.

A few had escaped, but most were taken from above.
The light wasn't gone. It was still searching.
It seemed to be searching for little Sammy.

Sammy pulled himself inside his shell.
He was too afraid to move.
Suddenly his shell lifted up off the ground.
His stomach swirled around and around.
Lightheaded and dizzy, Sammy's world started to fade.

 "UUUHHHHH!!!" yelled Sammy.
His scream woke him up from this very bad dream.
Yes, this was all just a very bad dream.
Wide awake, Sammy looked around.
He was still in Gracie's Garden,
   safe in the hollow between two rotting boards.

Sammy had dreamed this dream before.
He knew he would not be able to go back to sleep,
   so he stared at the walls and the ceiling above,
   and searched his memories for something about his past.

This place where he lived was falling apart.
The floor was rough and rocky and dirty.
The rotting wood walls were crumbling away.
The cardboard ceiling sagged so much,
   Sammy worried it might just collapse!

Sammy sighed as he slid back and forth.
  "Today is the day," he said out loud.
  "I have to find a better place to live."

Sammy packed a few small things,
  and stuffed them in his shell.

"I wish I could remember," he mumbled.
"Maybe the snails in my dream are real.
  Maybe I have a family somewhere.
  Maybe..... I have friends."

Sammy looked around.
  "I don't belong here in Gracie's Garden," he sighed.
  "No friends..... No family..... Nobody I can talk to.
  I just don't fit in. This place is not my home.
  I will not stay here anymore."

Sammy slid himself out of the lonely little hollow.
He left the rotting boards and the crumbling walls behind.
Outside, he looked across to the other side of the garden.
Moonlight lit up the great white garden gate.

  "I'm leaving Gracie's Garden!" declared Sammy.
  "I'm done with being sad and lonely and all by myself!
  It could be dangerous out there. It could be difficult.
  But how am I ever going to be happy,
    if I never take a chance for something new?"

Sammy slid slowly away into the beautiful moonlit garden.
He slid for several hours. A path of mulch led him forward.
Soft rays of sunlight began to light up the misty morning air.
Twinkling dew drops sparkled all around.
The Garden Center was getting closer.
There were just a few more curves to follow.

"What a beautiful morning," Sammy whispered to himself.

"Yes, it is," said a soft pretty voice.
"It's a very beautiful morning."

The voice startled Sammy.
He looked up to the top of the path rocks.
A small, painted, ceramic garden elf smiled down at him.
  "You can't talk," said Sammy.
  "You're a statue made of clay."

  "Hello, little Decollate snail!" said the sweet friendly voice.
  "I'm over here."

Sammy slid further around the bend.
Now, he could see the pretty little blue butterfly.
She was perched on top of the garden elf's nose.

  "Hi, my name is Bailey."

  "I know," said Sammy. "You are a very important butterfly."

  "Well, aren't you a smart little Decollate snail," laughed Bailey.

  "No, that's not me," blushed Sammy.
  "I just overheard Gracie talking in the garden.
    She always talks about how important you are.
    She says you help make the trees and flowers grow."

Sammy stopped to think for a moment.
  "What is a Decollate snail?" he asked.

"Well, you are!..... silly snail!" giggled Bailey.

Bailey fluttered her wings and lifted up,
   floating above the garden elf's nose.
"Decollate snail is what Gracie called you!
    I would love to talk more but I have to go.
        Welcome to Gracie's Garden!"
Then the pretty little butterfly fluttered away.

Sammy was curious.
He didn't know he was a Decollate snail.
So he wondered about this as he slid down the garden path.

Toward the Garden Center he went.
The great white garden gate was farther than it looked.
The sun grew hot as the morning slowly passed.
Sammy slid slowly around another curve.
Lucky for him, just ahead, lay a rotting hollow log.
This log rested on the ground in the shade,
   in the shade of Gracie's flowering shade vines.

Hot and tired, Sammy slid slowly into the log.
Snuggling into a cool, damp, rotting hollow knot, he rested.
He was hidden by a dangling door of moist green moss.
This was a perfect place for a snail to take a nap.

Sammy wondered about being a Decollate snail.
But he didn't wonder too long.
His tired eyes slowly shut,
   and here he fell asleep.
Most snails sleep during the day.

Chapter 2

When Sammy woke up, the sun was sound asleep.
He stretched his neck and pushed the hanging moss aside.
Sliding forward just a little, he peeked out.

A full moon glowed brightly over Gracie's Garden.
Tree shadows swayed in the moonlight.
A gentle breeze carried the smell of damp earth and mulch.
The fragrance of sleeping flowers tip-toed through the garden,
  and soft gentle music played with the shadows of a cricket.
It was such a peaceful place.

"HELLOOO!" shouted a loud, friendly voice.

The blur of wild rolling movement startled Sammy.
He pulled himself into his cracked little shell.

"HELLOOOO! WHAT are you hiding from in there?"

Slowly, Sammy peeked out of his snail shell.
In front of Sammy stood a roley poley with a big, friendly smile.

"HI! MY name is ROLEY ROANIN!
  WEL-come to MY hollow log!"

The little roley poley jumped into the air, flipped backwards,
  and landed with a big happy smile on his face.
He grabbed a chunk of rotting wood and stuffed it in his mouth.

"AND WHAT," laughed Roley, "is your name????"

"My name is Sammy.
  I didn't know this was your hollow log.
  I only needed a place to sleep.
  I can leave now."

The nervous little Sammy slid forward to leave.
  "I didn't mean to be any trouble," he said.

"NO! NO! NO! Do NOT leave here so quickly.
  I LOVE when company comes to visit.
  And THIS big hollow LOG has PLENTY of room.
  What did you say your name is again?"

"I am Sammy the Snail."

"A SNAIL??" huffed Roley Roanin.
"But you don't LOOK like a Garden Snail!" insisted Roley,
  "and you don't SOUND like a Garden Snail!"

Roley paused. He rolled his eyes upwards,
  all around and back down.

"MAYBE..... you are a small HERMIT CRAB!" he laughed.

"I am not a Hermit Crab," said Sammy.
"I am a snail."

Now, Roley Roanin was having fun.
  "But your shell isn't big, round and shiny like a Garden Snail.
    AND you are not bossy and mean like a Garden Snail."

Roley Roanin raised his right eyebrow.
A big smile stretched across his roley poley face.
  "MAAYYBBEE?..... you are a strange looking clam!"

"I am not a clam!" Sammy protested.
"I am a snail, but I am not a Garden Snail.
  I was just passing by on my way out of this lonely garden,
    and needed a place to rest."

"Well, as long as you are not a Garden Snail,
  sneaking around in the garden looking for a place to hide,
  while you make plans to eat up all of Gracie's beautiful
  flowering shade vines, then you are welcome to stay."

Roley Roanin curled up and spun around.
He stopped, stood up straight, and smiled big.
  "I'd like to stay and get to know you better,
    but I have other plans tonight and must be on my way.
    Nice meeting you, Sammy!"

The friendly little roley poley whirled around.
With a big smile and a loud, long "GOOD-BYYYE!!!!",
  Roley Roanin curled up into a ball and was gone in a blur.
Off he rolled into the moonlit shadows of Gracie's Garden.

Roley Roanin's speed surprised Sammy.
This roley poley simply disappeared.
And now, it was quiet again.

Sammy was alone in the knot of the empty hollow log.
Looking out, far beyond the dangling green moss, he sighed.
Moonlight and music reached out to touch the garden at night.
Sammy should have been on his way,
  but this spot was so peaceful and his eyes were still tired,
  so he slid back inside and went back to sleep.

Chapter 3

Morning came with a beautiful sunrise.
A soft, warm sunbeam woke Sammy from his sleep.
He had overslept.

This was a comfortable spot he had found.
But he knew this knot..... was not his home.
Sammy slid out and continued on his way.
However, once outside the hollow log, Sammy was lost.
He could not see the big white garden gate.
He must have gone the wrong way.

Sammy looked around and found a garden path close by.
Large square path rocks lined up along the edge.
Each of these rocks had a cool, damp shadow.
The shade of the path rocks was a perfect place to slide.
Traveling this new garden path was easy.
He passed another happy garden elf,
 and a shiny, green, glass frog.

Then, the big white garden gate reappeared.
Sammy was back on track.
Sammy slid. The hours passed by.
The sun climbed to the top of the sky.
The rocks on the path were losing their shadows,
  and Sammy's shell was getting hot.

A surprised Sammy slid past the next big rock.
A small picket fence traveled down the path.
Miniature red roses climbed up the posts.
Stepping stones and flowers led him to the gate.

Sammy poked his head between the pickets.
There he saw a perfectly cute country house.
The little blue and white house had fancy golden-yellow trim,
  and sunlight reflected off its pretty picture window panes.

On the front porch, a bench swing whispered to a rocking chair.
Colorful flowers frolicked below the front porch railing.
Stacked rocks climbed the chimney where smoke snuck out.
These puffs of smoke waved "hello" to Sammy.

The yard was just as pretty as the house.
Water twinkled and splashed around the ladybug fountain.
In the spray of the fountain, flower gardens danced.
Vegetable gardens marched along the side of the house.
Stepping stones walked from the porch stairs through the yard.
And the yard was neat and trim.

Just to see a real home made Sammy sad.
He wished he had a home of his own.

Chapter 4

"Hello."

A new voice startled Sammy.
He quickly lifted his head to look behind him,
  and bumped his head on the picket fence.

"OUCH!" said Sammy.

Behind him was a pretty little mouse.
She carried a basket of fresh raspberries.
  "I did not mean to scare you," she said.
  "That must have hurt."

"No, No, I'm fine. I was just leaving."

"My name is Maddy," said the pretty little mouse.
"It's nice to meet you.
  You must be Sammy!"

"Yes," said Sammy,
   "but how did you know my name?"

"I have a little roley poley friend," answered Maddy.
"His name is Roley Roanin. He came to visit me last night.
   Roley talked all about a little snail that came to visit him.
   And since you are quite obviously that snail,
      it must have been you."

Maddy smiled, "Let's go inside.
You shouldn't be out in this hot sun.
Snails are supposed to travel at night."

   "I wouldn't want to impose," said Sammy.

"It's no trouble at all," said Maddy.
"We can talk a little while you rest,
      and have something cool to drink.
   You can try one of my cocoa brownies.
   I cover them with sweet whipped cream,
      and fresh raspberries."

Maddy lifted up her little basket of raspberries,
 then opened the front gate.

Sammy nodded his approval of Maddy's very good idea.
He was hot and dry and hungry and tired and thirsty.
He slid through the open gate and followed her.
Across the stepping stones in the front yard, they went,
   then up three little stairs onto Maddy's front porch.
Through the front door and into the house, Maddy led the way.

This house was even prettier on the inside.
Pretty paintings of garden flowers covered the walls.
A rock fireplace in the front room was cool and quiet.
Fancy pieces of colored glass sparkled on the mantle.

To his right stood a wooden table and seven small chairs.
They all looked out through the pretty picture window panes.
The flower gardens and the water fountain were playing outside.

Beyond the table, a quaint country kitchen was cooking.
There were counter tops, a kitchen sink, with cabinets above.
Hot air wiggled out from a stove on the floor,
 as the smell of cocoa brownies traveled gently everywhere.

Ahead was an archway. It pulled Sammy forward.
Paints, brushes, easels and artist tables filled a great-room.
He saw paintings without frames and paintings half-finished.
Picture frames stacked themselves high in the corner.
A little wood chair stood stationary on the floor.
Its tiny wheels..... looked ready to roll.
Over the chair hung a little white painting smock,
 smudged with a rainbow of soft happy colors.

Maddy walked through the front room to the kitchen.
Looking over her shoulder, she called out to Sammy,
 "Please sit and make yourself comfortable."

Maddy opened her little oven and pulled out the brownies.
 "This is the perfect time for a visit," said Maddy.
 "These have just finished."

Sammy sat at the round wooden table.
This precious little house made him feel comfortable.
But it was Maddy who made him feel welcome.

Maddy talked as she decorated the delicious cocoa brownies.
She topped them with sweet whipped cream and red raspberries.
  "Roley Roanin tells me you are traveling," she said.
  "He says you are leaving Gracie's Garden."

  "Yes, I Am!" said Sammy trying to sound excited.
  "I am going on a great expedition to far away places."

  "Good for you!" said Maddy. "How exciting!"

And so they sat and they talked about Gracie's Garden,
  enjoying each other's company until late in the afternoon.
Then Maddy showed Sammy the guest room outside.
It was a comfortable space between the rocks.
Thick green leaves covered a bed of mulch and moss.
It was another great place for a snail to sleep.

  "Good night, Sammy," said Maddy.
  "Thanks for keeping me company.
    I'll have breakfast ready in the morning,
      then you can sleep all day tomorrow.
    Snails shouldn't travel in the heat of the day."

Sammy watched the little mouse walk back to her house,
  and up the front porch stairs.
  "Thanks for being so nice to me," he whispered.
Sammy pulled back into his shell and dozed off to sleep.

Chapter 5

After several hours of untroubled sleep, Sammy woke up.
He looked out from between the rocks.
Soft moonlight glowed on the house and gardens.
The little picket fence made him feel safe.
This was a perfectly peaceful place to be.

But Sammy did not believe,
  that Gracie's Garden could be his home.

  "It's time for me to go," he said.
  "I need to find a place where I belong,
      a place of my own.
    Maybe some day I will come back to visit.
    I can always come back to visit."

Sammy convinced himself.
Gracie's Garden was just not his home.
So he slid out of the little guest room and across the front yard.

Sammy quietly opened the gate and slid through,
  leaving the house and the pretty picket fence behind.
He traveled down the path of mulch.
It would be best to travel like most snails do,
  in the middle of the night.

Chapter 6

Maddy woke up at sunrise.
She washed and dressed and went down to the kitchen.
She pulled out some plates and quietly talked.

Who was she talking to?
A little mayfly on her window sill!

"I am going to make a nice breakfast for Sammy," she said.
"Maybe that will cheer him up. I know he's a lonely snail.
He tried to sound so happy and brave yesterday,
but he's not happy here in Gracie's Garden.
Roley Roanin told me how sad and lonely Sammy looked."

"Then after breakfast I will talk with Sammy.
I will ask him to stay here for awhile as my own special guest.
What do you think of that, little Mayfly?"

The little mayfly had nothing to say.

19

Maddy continued on.
  "We can have a 'Get to know Sammy' party!
  We will invite all the other garden animal friends.
  If Sammy knows he is welcome in Gracie's Garden,
    then he might want to make Gracie's Garden his home."

While Maddy talked,
  she put together a country garden breakfast:
  juice and berries and carrots and biscuits.
Of course, there was a plate of cocoa brownies too.

  "I am going to tell Gracie about Sammy being unhappy.
  She must have brought him to the garden for a reason,
    and she should know he is planning to leave."

The little mayfly sat quietly on the window sill.
She was a very good listener.

Maddy stepped out onto the front porch.
  "Sammy, I have breakfast ready for you," she called.

Sammy did not answer.
Maddy went down to the guest room to check on him.
The little Decollate snail was gone!

Maddy went to the backyard to look for him.
Then she went to the front yard.
She looked in the flower gardens, the vegetable gardens,
  and all around the house.
Then out the gate and onto the path she went.
Sammy was nowhere to be found.

She ran back through the gate and across the front yard.
Maddy bounded up the front porch stairs,
  then scurried past the bench swing and the rocking chair.

There, in the corner, hung an old rope from the porch ceiling.
With a tug and a pull, the emergency whistle sounded.
Then Maddy turned around and sat down.
There, in the rocking chair, she waited.

If she was going to find Sammy, she would need help.
And who are the very best ones to ask for help?
Your very best friends!

And they would soon be there!

Chapter 7

The whistle was heard whistling throughout Gracie's Garden.

The first friend to arrive was Bailey.
Her fancy butterfly wings flipped and fluttered.
Wings make traveling fast.

Bailey settled herself down on the front porch railing.
  "Am I the first to arrive?" she asked.

  "Of course," smiled Maddy.

At that very instant, a singing shadow fell from the sky.
    "IT'S… AAAAAAHH… T I I I I I E!"
Zacky the Cricket landed on a leaf in Maddy's front yard.
He grinned an intelligent grin.

Maddy laughed, "A tie? I don't think so!
  I do believe Bailey has beaten you again."

"Most Definitely A Tie!" declared Zacky.
"Hopping can be just as fast as flying.
  It depends upon the path you take!"

"My little grasshopper," said Maddy,
  "you are always so full of great wisdom."

Zacky responded with a smile.
  "Finding great wisdom and great luck,
    in a musical genius is rare.
    But the scientific world knows an insect with these qualities.
    That insect has been given a name: Acheta domesticus!
    Not..... I repeat NOT..... Little Grasshopper."

"Acheta domesticus?" asked Bailey and Maddy together.

Zacky enjoyed the confused look on their faces.
  "Yes, Acheta domesticus!" he said.
  "In simpler words..... A Cricket!"

Then Zacky chuckled,
  "I'm still convinced it was a tie."

Grinning his intelligent grin, Zacky looked around.
  "We seem to be missing some…"

But before Zacky could say "someone",
  a loud funny voice yelled out,

"WATCH OUT BELOWWWWWWWWWW!"

It came from above.
A blur of noisy movement catapulted through the air.
It flew across the front yard and into the ladybug water fountain.
All this interruption and confusion ended with a great big splash.

Up on the front porch, a few drops sprinkled down on Maddy.
Bailey quickly rose above the spray and stayed dry.
Zacky..... was sopping wet.

Chapter 8

"A warm HELLO to my dearly beloved friends!
And Hi to you, too..... Very Little Grasshopper!"

Roley Roanin winked at Zacky.
He enjoyed teasing his best friend in the whole world.

Zacky spoke firmly, "I am a Crick.....ettt!
NOT..... I repeat Not..... a very little grasshopper."

Then Zacky smiled as he wiped the water off his antennae.
"Little sea creature," he laughed,
"I do believe that was your best jump ever."

Roley stood up in the ladybug fountain and took a deep bow.
"Thank you! Thank you! Thank you!"

Roley Roanin looked sideways as he continued to bow.
"I am a land animal."

"Sea Creature," smiled Zacky

"Land Animal," grumbled Roley.

"Sea Creature," smiled Zacky.

And back and forth, they went.
"Land Animal!"
"Sea Creature!"
"Land Animal!"
"Sea Creature!"

"Now, Boys!" said Bailey.
"I'm sure that Maddy called us here for a good reason,
some better reason than to hear you two argue."

Zacky looked over at Roley and grinned.
"Oh? Like the last time she called us all to help.
Remember, the emergency birthday party!"

Roley Roanin giggled.
"Yeah, for a big old stinky box turtle with a crusty shell!
He was trespassing in our garden,
and it wasn't even his Birthday!"

"I still wonder who opened the gate," said Zacky.

Bailey interrupted them again.
"Nobody ever gave that sweet old turtle a birthday party.
Having that party at the garden gate stopped him there.
It stopped him from trampling over the whole garden."

"He could have injured my butterfly bushes.
    He could have ripped apart Maddy's little fence,
        and ruined this beautiful yard."

"Roley, that old turtle would have chewed up your hollow log.
    And Zacky, I believe turtles eat crickets.
    Maddy did us all a big favor."

"Thank you, Bailey," said Maddy.

Maddy grinned at Zacky and Roley.
    "This is much more important,
        than the old turtle's birthday party.
    I called you here because I need your help.
    But first, let me get you all some breakfast."

Roley laughed out loud.
    "Now, that's a great reason for sounding the emergency whistle!
    Might you have any of those famous cocoa brownies?"

Maddy smiled.
    "Absolutely!"

Chapter 9

Maddy brought her garden breakfast out to the front porch.
She told her three friends about Sammy the Snail's visit,
  and she told them about his plans to leave Gracie's Garden.

"Gracie did tell me," continued Maddy,
  "that she was bringing a new, special friend to the garden."

"Sammy must be Gracie's new special friend," said Zacky.
"If he's Gracie's special friend, he must be important."

Bailey spoke up to tell them what she knew.
"I heard Gracie talking to Sammy when he first arrived.
  Gracie told him that he was a very special kind of snail.
  She said one day he would help to keep the garden safe.
  Gracie called Sammy a Decollate snail.
  But, I'm pretty sure he did not hear her."

"Why is that?" asked Maddy.

"Sammy arrived in a small box," answered Bailey.
"When she opened it, I saw him.
   The opening to his shell was filled with thick sticky slime.
   He was sleeping."

While Bailey told them about Sammy, Roley Roanin ate.
Several cocoa brownies were crammed in his roley poley mouth.
He chewed and listened all at the same time.

Then, with his mouth full of brownies, Roley asked,
   "Wh- d-- --acie --ing su-- -n od- -ooking --ail to the gar--n?"
Roley's voice garbled. Lots of brownie crumbs fell out.

   "What did you say?" asked all his friends.

Roley quickly chewed.
He swallowed half the brownies in his mouth.
   "I said," Roley stopped to chew and swallow the other half.
   "Why did Gracie bring such an odd looking snail to the garden?
      Snails are always chewing up and slobbering
         on Gracie's plants, especially the fruit trees
         and berry bushes."

   "Yes, they are slobbery!" said Zacky.
   "Just like you with that big mouth full of brownies!"

Roley Roanin snatched the last cocoa brownie from the plate.
   "Well, snails ruin Gracie's Garden when they slobber.
   I'm just trying to help out one of my best friends.
   You know..... by getting rid of these old brownies."
Roley popped the last brownie in his mouth and smiled.

"I just made those brownies last night!" declared Maddy.
"THEY are NOT OLD!"

Roley Roanin continued to talk.
His mouth talked and chewed all at the same time.
  "Snails are big, bossy pests," he said,
    "and they eat everything in their slimy path.
    There are more and more of those Garden Snails every year.
    Maybe, they are plotting to take over Gracie's Garden.
    In my opinion, Garden Snails are good for nothing!"

  "All creatures have their purpose," Zacky reminded his friends.
  "Each and every creature..."

Roley Roanin quickly interrupted him.
  "Well, a friend of mine did say one good thing about them.
    Garden Snails are GOOD to EAT!
    But that's the only good thing I've heard about them."

  "Roley Roanin, you are correct," chuckled Zacky.
  "Too many Garden Snails are bad for Gracie's Garden.
    But this Sammy is a different kind of a snail.
    Just because he's a snail, doesn't mean he's a bad snail.
    Gracie must have a reason for bringing him to the garden."

  "What do you think we should do?" asked Bailey.

Maddy, Roley Roanin, and Bailey all looked at Zacky.
Thinking always turned Zacky quiet.
He thought for a few seconds.
Then, he spoke.

"We need to find this Sammy the Snail," said Zacky.
"We should stop him from leaving Gracie's Garden."

Zacky paused.
He sang an unusually high pitched musical note.
Zacky was always making strange musical sounds.

"We need to tell Gracie about Sammy," he continued.
"I have a plan. But it could be dangerous."

For a few moments, the four friends stood silently together.
It was the silence that let them first hear the sound.
The sound was a buzzing sound.

Now, buzzing sounds in the garden can be good,
  or buzzing sounds in the garden can be bad.

The four friends moved quickly and quietly.
They crouched behind the corner of Maddy's house.
The buzzing sound grew louder.
The four friends stayed out of sight.

Then, all of a sudden, Zacky hopped.
He hopped high up into the air over Maddy's front yard.
He disappeared into bright sunlight.
The three friends gasped when they heard the crashing sounds,
  and they rushed out from behind the house.

Up in the air over Maddy's front yard,
  a tangle of buzzing wings and cricket legs fell from the sky.
Zacky and the enemy struggled.

Roley Roanin picked up the broken tip of a sharp nail.
Shaking it like a sword, Roley ran through the yard.
 "I will save you!" he yelled as loudly as he could.

Maddy rushed out after him.
She held in her hand a very sharp sewing needle.
She slashed the needle through the air in front of her.
Maddy could be a very protective little mouse.
Anyone attacking her or her peaceful friends would pay dearly.

Bailey knew she had to help her friends.
She flew up into the air and spread her butterfly wings.
She blocked out the glaring sunlight.
Now, her friends could see the enemy.

Roley Roanin and Maddy rushed out to save Zacky,
 but the battle was already done.
The struggling stopped.
Everything was quiet.

The enemy lay lifeless on the ground.
And there, beside the enemy, silent and still,
 lay Zacky's limp body.

Chapter 10

Roley Roanin and Maddy held their weapons steady.
No sound or movement came from the enemy or Zacky.
Bailey hovered above them.
The three friends were stunned.

Then, the laughing started.
Zacky laughed hysterically.
The enemy buzzed with laughter too.
It was a gentle, buzzing laughter.

Zacky stood up and took a deep bow.
  "Let me introduce to you an old friend of mine," he said.
  "This is Buster Bumbler, the Great Bumbling Bumble Bee."

  "Hello," said the old bumble bee.
  "It is an honor to meet you.
    I apologize if I frightened you in any way.
    I did not know Zacky was here with friends."

37

"It's a pleasure to make your acquaintance," smiled Maddy.
"And not to worry, this mouse enjoys a good practical joke."

Roley Roanin however, was not so quick to forgive.
He chased after Zacky waving his little sword wildly in the air.
  "You dim-witted little grasshopper!" thundered Roley.
  "You Scared The Girls!"

Zacky jumped out of the way.
  "Not a Grasshopper!" he laughed
  "But at least I know you still care about me, Sea Creature!"

Roley chased Zacky around the yard.
Swinging his little sword back and forth, he yelled,
  "Let's see how far a one-legged garden cricket can jump."

  "Stop playing games you silly bugs," scolded Bailey.
  "We have important things to do."

Bailey flew down to meet and greet Buster Bumbler.
Roley Roanin calmed down and stopped chasing Zacky.
Zacky hopped next to Maddy. She would protect him.
Maddy let the tip of her sewing needle fall to the ground.

Buster Bumbler turned to Zacky.
  "You called for me?" asked Buster Bumbler.

After a moment of silence, Zacky spoke.
  "Bumbler, thanks for coming so quickly this morning.
  We have a problem here in Gracie's Garden.
  I think we are going to need your help."

Chapter 11

Sammy had left a long time before sunrise.
He did not want to be a burden or ask for help.
And he did not want anyone trying to change his mind.

Quietly, he opened the little picket fence gate.
Out he went, traveling down the mulch path.
The morning sun lifted slowly.

He slid in the shade of the wall made of path rocks.
Between these rocks were small, safe, shady places to rest.
But as the sun climbed higher, even these places lost their shade.
By noon time, it was just too hot. The sun was drying him out.
Sammy was weak and his slime was getting sticky.
He struggled past the edge of the next big path rock.
  "Maybe there will be some shade," hoped Sammy.

He turned past the next rocky edge and gasped,
  "I can't believe my very good luck!"

Between the next two path rocks was a gap.
These path rocks were not touching at all.
The tall shady rock walls loomed over the little snail.
Sammy slid between the rocks and through to the other side.

There, he found a cool, damp, shady, garden path.
This was a path a snail could travel, even during the day.
Sammy looked up past the leaves of the shade plants.
Ahead, in the distance, stood the big white garden gate.
This new path seemed to travel straight to it.

Feeling lucky, Sammy slid slowly on his way.
The hours passed and the sun began to set.
As the daylight faded to darkness,
  strange shadows danced across his path.
Unusual sounds spooked the little snail.
Sammy felt lost and a little bit scared.

Sammy spied a leaf. It was leaning over, touching the ground.
  "That leaf looks like a good place to stop," he mumbled.

Quietly, he wiggled over to the leaf.
Sammy was just about to slide under, when it started to shake.
The shaking leaf shook louder as it rose up into the air.
Two huge orange-yellow eyes looked out.
They both looked right at Sammy.

He tried to slide back and away from the scary eyes,
  but he was much too afraid to move.
Sammy was stuck, shaking with fear.
Sammy the Snail was honestly scared!

Chapter 12

Zacky, what a genius!
Thinking, organizing, and planning,
  he spent the morning drawing a large map of Gracie's Garden.
Maddy's front room was Zacky's headquarters.

  "We need to find Sammy," said Zacky pointing to the map.
  "He's an odd-shaped little snail with a cracked shell,
    and he was last seen here."

Zacky pointed to a picture on the map.
It was a picture of Maddy's little country house.

  "Maddy was the last one to speak with him," continued Zacky.
  "That was yesterday afternoon about three o'clock.
    Maddy checked the guest room at half past seven this morning.
    Sammy was gone. He must have left sometime last night.
    Snails like to travel after dark. It was dark at nine o'clock.
    If he left at nine, he has a twelve hour head start."

41

Roley Roanin looked at Maddy.
 "How fast can a snail travel?" he asked.

Maddy looked perplexed.
 "I'm not sure," she answered.

"Most snails travel ten to fifteen feet in an hour," said Zacky.
 "The fastest snail can move about forty feet in an hour."

Being good at math, Bailey figured it out.
 "That means Sammy could have gone 480 feet!" she said.
 "He could be out of the garden by now."

"Yes," said Zacky, "but Sammy is not the fastest kind of snail.
 And there are only a few ways in and out of Gracie's Garden.
 Most likely, Sammy is still in the garden."

Maddy spoke up,
 "Gracie's Garden can be a dangerous place for a snail.
 Birds, ground beetles, glowworms and caterpillars-
 All of them enjoy having a snail for dinner."

"Maddy is correct," said Zacky.
 "We have to find Sammy before they do,
    and we will need all the help we can get."

Zacky looked over at Roley Roanin.
 "Roley, will you contact all of your roley poley friends?
 We need to start a ground search for little Sammy.
 We need to search the entire garden."

With two of his right hands, Roley Roanin saluted Zacky.
  "Yes, Sir! Immediately!" he shouted.
  "We are at your service, General Grasshopper!"

Zacky smiled at Roley's enthusiasm, and the grasshopper joke.

Continuing to stand at attention, Roley clearly announced:
  "Sir, I will have the roley poley troops move out at once.
  It will be the greatest ground search in history.
  We will roll over every inch of Gracie's Garden.
  The roley poleys will leave no stones unturned.
  ...Except the Heavy Ones!"

  "Very Good," said Zacky.
  "Here's a small map of the garden paths and trails.
  Be careful in the areas marked with a black S.
  Those are snake holes."

  "Sir! We are not afraid of snakes! Sir!" snapped Roley.

  "Just stay away from the snake holes," smiled Zacky.

Then Zacky looked to Bailey.
  "Bailey, you can see things that we cannot.
  Those beautiful wings can carry you across the garden.
  Will you check the few ways in and out of the garden?
  We need to know if Sammy finds his way out.
  With your help, we might find him before it's too late."

Bailey answered with her soft sweet butterfly voice.
  "I always help my friends if the help is for something good!"

Zacky turned to Maddy.
"Maddy, we need you to visit the big white house on the hill.
Gracie should know that Sammy is leaving.
Only you know all the rooms inside Gracie's house.
Only you can find Gracie and bring her here."

"All I need is my backpack," said Maddy,
"and I'm ready to go."

"It's a difficult and dangerous mission," warned Zacky.
"You will have to be extremely quick and very careful.
And at all times, watch out for that big, black cat, Magic."

Maddy smiled, "I will definitely be packing my sewing needle!"

Each of the four friends were anxious to get started.
They gave each other hugs and handshakes.

Zacky pulled Roley Roanin over to him.
He gave him a tight hug and a slap on the back.
"You be extra careful, my little sea creature.
There are dangerous places in Gracie's Garden,
places where no roley poleys have ever been.
Stay away from funnel spiders!"

Roley Roanin laughed.
"Do you really think a funnel spider could catch
the Fastest Roley Poley in the Universe?
I thought you were a WISE little grasshopper."

Roley winked at Zacky, curled up and rolled away in a blur.

Zacky shouted as he watched Roley go.
"Be careful, little sea creature!"

Then Zacky and Maddy hugged Bailey goodbye.
They waved and smiled thanks as she fluttered away.

Zacky put his hand on Maddy's shoulder.
"I want you to be extra careful," he said.
"I know you understand how dangerous your mission will be,
    but take No Chances around That Cat."

"Thank you for the concern," said Maddy.
"It's really very sweet."

Maddy flashed her sewing needle through the air.
"Don't worry. I'm quite able to take care of myself."

"I am sending Buster Bumbler with you," said Zacky.
"He can watch for Magic from the air."

Maddy smiled and gave Zacky a big hug,
  then went to pack for her trip.

Still, Zacky was concerned.
That's exactly why he called Buster Bumbler.

Zacky crawled over to Bumbler's side and talked quietly.
  "Thank you, Bumbler, for answering my call.
    We need you to watch out for Maddy.
    You can see things from the air that she can not.
    Try your best to keep her away from that big, black cat."

"I am honored to be called on by an old friend," said Bumbler.
"It's been a long time since I've been called to duty.
  You remember, I was a general in the Bumble Bee Army.
  I will take this dangerous mission very seriously.
  Zacky, you can count on me."

"Yes, that's for sure," thought Zacky.

General Buster Bumbler was a famous hero.
...Won his general's stripes in the great Bee Wars.
He and his soldiers crushed invading troops of killer bees.

Despite his age,
  this bumble bee still had lots of zing and sting left in him.

"Thank you again, Bumbler," said Zacky.
"You're a true and trusted friend!"

Chapter 13

Sammy shook with fear.
In front of him, were the scariest eyes he had ever seen.
He wished he had never left his little hollow,
  that safe place between two rotting boards.

  "Hello," said Sammy with his scared and shaky voice.
  "Hello, my name is Sammy."

The scary eyes did not answer him.
They moved slowly forward toward Sammy.
The big leaf shook.

Terrified, Sammy wrenched himself into his shaking shell.
  "Please don't eat me," he cried.

The big leaf shook more and more as the monster,
  with its big scary eyes, moved toward him.
There was nothing Sammy could do.

Sammy was sure. This was the end.
He would never have a home of his own,
  and never feel warm sunlight on his shell again.

The eyes moved closer.
The great leaf shook louder.
Sammy felt weak in his stomach and very lightheaded.
He watched the monster's big, dark mouth open wide,
  and then the monster's mouth fell toward him.

Sammy's head was spinning.
It only took a moment for the monster's mouth to fall.
Sammy's world turned black and silent.

Chapter 14

Maddy and Buster Bumbler talked as they walked.
Down the big, garden path of mulch, they went.
Maddy explained about the garden.

"There are only a few ways to get into Gracie's Garden,
  and only a few ways out," she said.

"I can buzz into the garden anytime," said Bumbler.
"The netting screen is open at the Garden Center."

"Yes, you can, Mr. Bumbler,
  and so can our good friend Bailey.
  But little animals without wings find that way very dangerous.
  Climbing on the inside of the netting screen is not so scary.
  Climbing on the outside of the screen is a problem.
  Birds like to eat small animals that climb on the screen."

"Well, there must be some way out of the garden," said Bumbler.

"Gracie's father put up the netting screen," said Maddy.
"The screen covers almost all of Gracie's Garden.
 It keeps out most of the small pests that live in other gardens.
 There is also a hard-wire screen behind the white picket fence.
 The hard-wire screen is buried down into the ground.
 It keeps out dogs, cats, rats and even rabbits.
 Gracie's Garden is a very safe place."

"If the garden gate is locked," said Bumbler.
"Then we have no way out!"

"We could get out through a snake hole," said Maddy,
   "but that's a very dangerous way to go.
 A big, black snake lives in those holes.
 He is always happy to see little animals.
 I bet you can guess why!"

"I wonder if snakes eat bumble bees?" Bumbler asked himself.
He couldn't remember a bumble bee eaten by a snake.

"Snakes enjoy eating all kinds of creatures," answered Maddy.
"But most of all, they like to eat little country mice."

"We had better stay away from the snake hole!" said Bumbler.

"I think that's a good idea," agreed Maddy.

Buster Bumbler and Maddy reached the garden gate.
They both looked up.
The tall, white garden gate reached to the sky.
There seemed to be no way out.

Bumbler knocked on the hard, white wooden gate.
  "Then how do you plan to get out of the garden?" he asked.

  "With this!" squeaked Maddy.
She pulled a very small gold key from her backpack.

Buster Bumbler looked at Maddy with surprise.
  "That small key can't possibly open this big white garden gate."

Maddy giggled at such a silly idea.
Of course this little key wouldn't open the enormous gate.
  "This little key belonged to my father," she said.
  "He was a scientific mouse. He worked for Gracie's father.
    My father was very smart about gates and locks and keys.
    Gracie gave this key to him on his very first day in the garden.
    He used to dangle it above my bed when I was just a baby.
    Then he would say, that I was the one true key to his heart."

Maddy rubbed her little hands against the garden gate.
She pushed on a small wooden panel.
This small wooden panel slid to the side and disappeared.
Behind it was a secret door made of gold and copper and silver.
Maddy put the tiny key into the door's lock and turned it.
The little door clicked open.

On the other side of the door was another wooden panel.
Maddy slid this one open, too.
She and Buster Bumbler stepped through.
Now, they stood outside Gracie's Garden.
Maddy slid the panels back into place,
  and locked the fancy little door.

This was not the first time Maddy had been out of the garden,
  but it was the first time without Gracie.

"Let's go," said Maddy; her voice filled with excitement.
"We need to move quickly and quietly."

Maddy started out at a run.
This was probably the most dangerous part of the trip.
She was out in Gracie's big, front yard,
  out in the open with no place to hide.

Buster Bumbler buzzed through the air above her.
  "I am watching out for you, Maddy," said Bumbler.

He buzzed back and forth and all over the front yard.

"And all I have is very good news," he mumbled to himself.
"There is no sign of that big, black cat!"

Chapter 15

Sammy the Snail woke up.
Which means, he must have fainted.
You know..... passed out!

It was pitch black dark. He couldn't see a thing.
He should have been all eaten up by now, but he wasn't.
Or maybe he was eaten up, and this was Snail Heaven.
Or maybe he was having just another bad dream.

The last thing Sammy remembered was the monster.
Those big, scary, yellow-orange eyes frightened him.
The monster's eyes had come closer and closer and closer.
Then the monster's big, dark mouth fell toward him.
He must have been eaten.

Sammy shuddered as he stretched out his neck.
He blinked his eyes, but still couldn't see a thing.
He tried to move, but his shell was stuck to the ground.

"Hello, can anyone hear me?" whispered Sammy.
No one answered.

"Can anyone help me?" he asked a little louder.
"I seem to be stuck. Hellooo!
  Is anyone there?"

Sammy spoke even louder, "Where is this Place?"

Suddenly, the yellow-orange monster eyes reappeared.
Sammy was scared all over again.
He pulled himself back into his shell,
  then, slowly and cautiously peeked out just a little.

The glowing eyes stared down at him.
The monster's face was black and scaly,
  and it seemed to be wiggling all over.

Sammy looked at the dark hole of the monster's mouth.
The mouth was open but there were no teeth.
This strange looking monster had no body at all.
Sammy had never seen any creature that looked so ugly.

Then deep in the monster's mouth, a light appeared.
It was a bright light..... a white light.
The light moved toward Sammy.

Now Sammy could see the room that held him.
Above him, the roof was made of thick, brown leaves.
The floors and the walls were made of dirt.
Ropes of twine held his shell to the ground.

Sammy could see the monster in front of him.
The monster's face..... little wiggling black spots.

As the light grew brighter, he saw what they were.
This monster was not really a monster at all.
The little wiggling black spots were lightning bugs.
This monster was made out of lightning bugs.

These lightning bugs were pretending.
The "monster's" glowing eyes,
  were made with the lights of the fireflies.
This monster was just one big scary trick.

Sammy looked back towards the light.
The bright, white, shining light surrounded him.
But then, the brightness of the light dimmed.
It was enough for Sammy to see her outline.
In front of him stood the figure of a Queen.

  "I am Maggie," she said.
  "I am Queen of the Glowworms."

Sammy shuddered.
He clearly heard her say glowworms.
Glowworms eat snails.

Her voice was calm, confident and commanding.
Yet, it was also soft and beautiful.
  "You are a special snail," said the Queen.
  "And, for now, you are our prisoner."

Sammy began to think.
He did not want to be the prisoner of anyone.
...Especially lightning bugs.

Lightning bugs lay tiny eggs.
Those tiny eggs grow up to be glowworms.
And Glowworms Are Always Hungry!
...Hungry for snails!

Sammy didn't want to be eaten.
He felt weak in his stomach and very lightheaded.
Everything started spinning again.
Sammy's world went black and silent.
He fainted..... again!

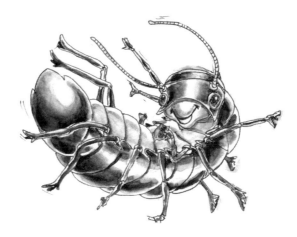

Chapter 16

Roley Roanin rolled ahead of the others.
Ten groups of roley poleys rolled through Gracie's Garden.
They started the search for Sammy in the upper garden.
Now, he and his friends were in the middle garden.

Roley Roanin sped along raising up a trail of dust.
He was on his way back to headquarters.
It was time to tell Zacky what they had found.
So far there was no sign of Sammy.

He decided to take the old trail.
Instead of going straight back, he would search The Edge.
At The Edge, Roley could look out over the lower garden.
Then he could take a shortcut trail back to Maddy's house.

He was almost to the lookout point.
Maybe his very good luck would help him find Sammy.
Roley Roanin rolled faster as he thought about.....

"BOOM!!! CRASH!!!"

"ROLEY POLEY POOH!" screamed Roley.
He came to a screeching halt.

A huge flower, much bigger than a baseball,
  fell right across the old trail.
Roley Roanin had almost been smashed flat and dead.
He was lucky his reflexes were as fast as his rolling.
Roley grumbled out loud to himself,
  "Gracie is not going to be very happy about this!"

He studied the flower and its broken petals.
  "It's a good thing I am an expert at climbing," he said.
  "This will be some extra fun! How lucky is that?"

He easily climbed to the top of the big red flower ball.
On top, Roley Roanin could see.
He could see exactly what caused the great flower to fall.
  Garden Snails!
He saw hundreds of them.
They were destroying Gracie's Garden,
  chomping every flower, plant and fruit tree.
Behind them was nothing left but slobbering slime.

  "WHO GOES THERE?" shouted a loud commanding voice.

Below him on the path were several big, mean-looking snails.
These slimy, stinky Garden Snails looked up at him.

  "COME DOWN HERE RIGHT NOW!" yelled the biggest one.

"Who is going to make me?" Roley hollered back.
"You or your slobbering sidekicks?"

"We have orders to place all insects under arrest," said a guard.

"Good thing I'm not an insect!" howled Roley.
"I am a Roley Poley!"

"You are under Arrest!" yelled the Garden Snail guards.

"Roley Poleys are crustaceans!" yelled Roley.
"IF you had gone to school, you would know that.
 Everyone knows that crustaceans are not insects!
 Did your boss say anything about arresting,
            CRUST-A-CEANS?"

Roley Roanin giggled to himself. These snails looked confused.
They definitely did not know what a crustacean was,
 and they probably didn't want to get into trouble,
 for arresting the wrong guy.

Roley Roanin waved at the stinky Garden Snails,
 then showed them his biggest and friendliest smile.

 "SEE YA! ..... Wouldn't Want to BE YA!"

Roley jumped in the air and rolled down the flower stem.
He headed straight for the Garden Snail guards.
At the last second, he turned sharply to the left.
He rolled into a curled flower petal and disappeared.
Half a millisecond later, Roley shot out.

The curled tip of the flower petal sent him flying through the air.
He soared right over the Garden Snails onto the old trail,
  and left the stinky snails in a trail of roley poley dust.
No snail in the world could ever come close to catching him.
He was sooooooo fast!

Roley Roanin was on his way.
Soon he would be telling Zacky all about these Garden Snails.
He sped down the old trail toward the Old Dirt Patch.

  "Almost there," he said proudly to himself.

He turned off the trail and rolled into a clearing.
Nothing grew here except roots and rocks.
Drain water washed everything else away.
This was the Old Dirt Patch.

  "I wouldn't want to be here in a rainstorm!" laughed Roley.

At the end of the Old Dirt Patch was a small cliff.
There, an old white plastic pipe stuck out.
This pipe drained water away from the Garden Center.

Climbing over roots and rocks, Roley made his way up.
Soon he was at the opening of the drain pipe.
Roley peeked around the edge and looked inside.
It was dark, but there was no movement in the pipe.
It was empty except for a few stones about halfway through.

Roley Roanin climbed in and headed up the pipe.
  "Best shortcut in the garden," he said out loud to himself.

"It works well for us too," laughed the voices of snails.

The smooth stones in the pipe transformed.
These stones were not stones at all.
This was a trap!

Roley quickly rolled back down the pipe.
At the end of the pipe, Roley Roanin snapped open,
  and soared through the air.

He landed in the middle of the dirt patch below.
There, he stopped and stood up straight.
Big round smooth stones transformed all around him.
Garden Snails filled the entire clearing,
  and completely surrounded Roley Roanin.

This..... was a very good trap.

Chapter 17

Zacky sat atop the spout of the watering can,
  listening to the chatter of insects and other animals.
Still, there was no word of Sammy.

Bailey's butterfly wings fluttered.
She settled down next to Zacky.

  "What are you sitting around for?" she asked.

  "I am waiting for a pretty little butterfly," he smiled.
  "She is supposed to meet me here at exactly four O'clock.
   And MY sundial says one minute after four O'clock!
   She's late."

  "Well, if you have been waiting for THIS pretty little butterfly,
       then your time has been well spent," she said.
  "I'm here!"

63

"Did you spy anything interesting from the air?" asked Zacky.

"I did not see Sammy," answered Bailey.
"But there are Garden Snails everywhere in the lower garden.
  Flowers are falling to the ground. Gracie's plants look sick.
  Something bad is happening."

"Garden Snails invading the garden..... not good," said Zacky.
"I will bring news to the lightning bugs. They should know."

"What about Sammy?" asked Bailey.

"We must keep looking for him," answered Zacky.
"Let's meet again tonight at seven on Maddy's front porch.
  Roley Roanin should be back by then too.
  And Bailey, thank you for all your hard work and help."

"I am happy to help," smiled Bailey.
"I will do my best to see what can be seen.
  And of course next time, I will try to be on time.
  You know how unpredictable flying can be."

Zacky smiled, "It's an honor to have you as my friend.
  If only others in the world were as responsible as you are,
     and worked half as hard as you do.
  Your help is truly appreciated."

Bailey blushed as she took off into the air.
  "You talk too much, Little Cricket!" she giggled back.
Then Bailey the Butterfly fluttered away.
She continued to search for little Sammy.

Chapter 18

Maddy darted across the big front yard.
Buster Bumbler buzzed overhead.

"I'm always a little bit nervous in open areas," she said.

Buster cleared his throat.
"It's much easier to fly. If only you had a pair of wings."

Maddy laughed at the thought of having wings.
"I don't think people would like a flying mouse," said Maddy.
"Gracie tells me that running mice are chased with broomsticks.
A flying mouse could be quite dangerous."

Bumbler chuckled back,
"Broomsticks swinging in the air does sound dangerous,
but having wings would help you stay away from cats."

"Cats are what we mice fear the most!" said Maddy.

Cats..... just saying the word made her a little bit nervous.
Maddy began to run more quickly through the yard.

Bumbler followed overhead.
  "Sprays of all kinds are what we bees fear the most," he said.
  "A bee sprayer will paralyze a bee instantly."

  "Have you ever been sprayed?" asked Maddy.

  "No," said Bumbler,
   "but my cousin was hit by a sprayer.
  He was hit from over forty feet away.
  He never saw it coming.
  It was such a horrible sight.
  First, he went blind, yelling, 'I can't see! I can't see!'
  Then his wings started sputtering on and off.
  It was a horrible sound like this,
  'UNMM! pata pata, UNMM! pata pata, Unmm pata pata.'
  He was swirling and looping in the air.
  Then, he fell from the sky."

Bumbler's wings started making horrible sounds.
Maddy slowed down and looked up to see what was wrong.
He was flying in strange circles, out of control.
Then Buster Bumbler fell toward the ground.

Maddy ran faster toward the falling Bumbler.
She tried to catch him, but Bumbler hit the ground.
He was there in front of her at the edge of the first rock wall,
  making very loud noises and shaking all over.
Then the noises and the shaking stopped.

"Are you all right Mr. Bumbler?" asked Maddy.
She gently poked the old general.

Buster Bumbler jumped up smiling.
  "Why, of course I'm alright!" he buzzed.
  "I just thought we should take some time to rest."
Bumbler brushed himself off.
He looked right at Maddy.
  "So, did you think I was dead?"

Maddy giggled at the old bumble bee.
  "Zacky told me you might show off your acting skills.
    He said you were almost famous at the China Bee Theatre.
    I think your death fall was spectacular!"

  "Why, thank you," said Bumbler, humbly taking a bow.

  "It sure is nice to be out of the open field," said Maddy.
  "And I'm not tired at all. Let's keep moving."

Maddy began to climb.
Buster Bumbler flew up over the rock wall.
He looked for danger.
He looked for the big black cat.

  "The first level looks safe," he said.
  "No sign of the cat!"

Maddy finished climbing,
  and crossed the first level of the yard quickly.
Then she began climbing a second wall of stacked rocks.

Close by, she saw rock stairs.
  "It's much easier for me to climb this wall," she thought.
  "Stairs are too tall and slippery for a mouse to climb."

Maddy continued jumping from rock to rock.
Bumbler buzzed back again.
  "Just one more level of landscape rocks," he said.
  "The next level looks safe too."

Maddy reached the second level and darted across.
They reached the last wall of stacked rocks.
Bumbler buzzed up and over to look for danger.

Maddy was already climbing when Bumbler returned.
  "Stop climbing," he whispered.
  "Magic is napping in the empty bird bath."

Maddy looked gratefully at Bumbler and whispered back.
  "I'm sure glad I've got you to watch out for me.
    Is there any way to get past?"

  "I buzzed around up there," answered Bumbler.
  "There is no way past Magic if you climb this wall,
      but there is a black drainpipe close to the front door.
    That pipe goes underground."

  "The other end must come out somewhere," said Maddy.
  "Maybe the other end of the drainpipe is somewhere close by.
    Will you look for it?"

  "Of course!" said Bumbler.

Bumbler buzzed off.
He came back in a few minutes.
  "I found the same kind of drainpipe," he said quietly,
    "hidden behind a piece of shiny copper metal.
  The pipe is sticking out of the rock wall.
  It goes underground just like the other one.
  Follow me."

Maddy followed Bumbler along the wall, under a bush,
  and then behind a sheet of shiny copper metal.
There, a deep ditch lay between the metal and the rock wall.
A black plastic drainpipe stuck out of the wall.

Maddy leapt across the ditch to the rock wall.
Up and over the top of the black drainpipe, she climbed.
Then she jumped down, landing on the top of the pipe.
Carefully, she walked out to the end and looked over.
The dangerously deep ditch looked even deeper from up there.
Maddy flipped herself over the edge and into the pipe.

She looked into the pipe, then back out at Buster Bumbler.
  "This pipe travels upwards underground.
    If this end connects to the end near Gracie's front porch,
      then it shouldn't take me long to get there.
    Will you wait for me at the other end?
    It shouldn't take more than a few minutes."

"I will wait for you no matter how long it takes," said Bumbler.
  "But remember to be careful!
    Drainpipes are dangerous!"

Maddy pulled out her sewing needle.
She winked at the old bumble bee.

"I'll see you in a little bit!" she smiled.

She slashed her sewing needle through the air, turned around,
  climbed up into the pipe, and disappeared.

Chapter 19

Sammy was alive.
When he woke up, ropes still held him down.
The lightning bugs had moved their prisoner to a different place.
Sammy looked around the small round room.
Two firefly guards watched over him.

"Where am I?" asked Sammy.

The smaller of the two guards replied stiffly.
"This a holding room," he said.
"We are below the Great Glowworm Meeting Hall.
Senior members of the firefly council are meeting there now.
They are trying to decide what is to be done with you.
No harm will come to you at this time.
We will not answer any more questions."

Dim light glimmered down from the center of the ceiling.
Soft yellow light bounced around on the polished wood walls.

These wood walls curved around him in a circle.
This little room had no cracks or corners or windows or doors.
There did not seem to be any way in..... or any way out.

"Where am I?" asked Sammy.
"Are we still in Gracie's Garden?
  How did we get in here?
  Why are there no doors or windows?
  What are you going to do with me?
  Can I speak to somebody in charge?"

But the firefly guards stood still,
  and did not answer.

Sammy asked again, "Can I talk to someone in charge?"

The firefly guards stood still.
They did not answer.

Chapter 20

" ONE!   TWO!   THREE! "
Roley Roanin counted the snails slowly, pointing to each one.
  "Four, Five, Six, Seven,"
With every snail, he counted more quickly.
  "Eight, nine, ten, eleven, twelve, thirteen, fourteen, fifteen..."

He counted faster and faster until almost all the Garden Snails
  in the clearing were counted, then he slowed down again.
  "Fifty-nine, Sixty,   Sixty-ONE,   SIXTY----- TWO!"

Roley Roanin finished counting.
  "Who's in charge here?" he asked.
  "Do you have a leader?"

Not one of the Garden Snails answered him.

  "Do you have a leader?" he asked again.
  "You Know! A BOSS?"

The snail soldiers plodded slowly toward Roley Roanin.
These tough looking Garden Snails completely surrounded him.
Roley watched a large fancy shell move toward him.

From behind the soldiers, a big Grove snail slid forward.
  "I am General Nemoralis," said the big Grove snail.
  "I am in charge of this snail army."

  "A Snail??" asked Roley Roanin.
  "But your face doesn't look like a Garden Snail.
    And you don't sound like a Garden Snail.
    Maybe you are a small Hermit Crab!"

The General retorted with a flash of anger.
  "I am not a Hermit Crab! I am a Grove Snail!
    And I am in charge of this snail army!"

Roley Roanin stretched out his smile,
  and raised an eyebrow up in the air.
  "BUT your shell doesn't look like a Garden Snail!
    AND you are bossier and meaner than a Garden Snail.
    MAAYYYBBEE..... you are a strange looking clam?"

  "I am not a clam!" rumbled General Nemoralis.
  "I am the GENERAL in charge of this army!
    And I demand respect from my prisoners!"

Roley Roanin stood up straight and saluted.
  "YES SIR!" he shouted.

Then Roley's face twisted into a look of confusion.

Roley Roanin let his saluting hands fall.
  "SIR, there is only one little problem," he said.

"And What Is THAT?" shouted General Nemoralis.

Roley Roanin answered with a most quiet and gentle voice.
  "I am not a prisoner."

General Nemoralis looked at Roley with surprise.
  "I have you surrounded by over sixty of my best snail soldiers.
  I am in command of the largest snail army ever created.
  All INSECTS in this garden are to be captured.
  YOU ARE MY PRISONER!!!" he roared.

Roley Roanin stretched his arms up into the air,
  and rested them gently on his head.
  "UMMM? No I'm Not! And by the way,
  I am not an insect. I am a crustacean.
  Most people get that wrong too.
  I am actually kind of like a very small lobster.
  Most of my cousins live in the ocean,
    but that's pretty far away and..."

"SILENCE!" screamed the general.

But Roley Roanin continued talking quietly to the soldiers.
  "My cousins live deep in the sea.
  There are lots of strange animals that live there.
  Some are as big as an oak tree, and they have teeth."

"Seize Him Now!" commanded the general to his troops.

Roley Roanin rolled up into a ball.
He started to roll in a tight circle.
Faster and faster, he rolled.

"COMING THROUGH!" Roley laughed loudly.

He hit the first soldier's snail shell with a POP!
Roley's hard crustacean shell bounced off the soldier's shell.
He hit the next soldier even harder and faster.
POP!   POP!   POP!
POP! POP! POP! POP! POP!
POP!POP!POP!POP!POP!POP!POP!POP!
Roley moved like a pinball in a pinball machine.
Each POP! moved him faster and faster.
He knocked into one snail soldier after another.

"SEIZE HIM NOW!" yelled the general.

Roley Roanin rolled back, straight toward the general.
He was rolling sooooo fast!

"Now I'VE GOT YOU!" snarled General Nemoralis.

The general tried to grab Roley Roanin.
But Roley Roanin tightened up.
He shrunk himself just enough.
He rolled right under the general's stretched out folds.

"See Ya..... Wouldn't want to Bee Ya!"

Roley Roanin rolled right up the curves of the general's shell.
Then up and over the general's head, he went.
As Roley Roanin shot up and away and into the air,
  he knocked off the general's helmet.

Always polite, Roley yelled back,
        "SORRY!"
  as he soared over all the snail soldiers,
  and landed in the drainpipe shortcut.

There was no stopping him now.
General Nemoralis struggled up the cliff of dirt and rock.
He looked into the opening of the pipe.
It was empty.
Roley Roanin was gone.

General Nemoralis, angry and frustrated, yelled into the pipe.
  "I am going to get you, little bug.
   I AM GOING TO GET YOU!"

General Nemoralis calmed himself down.
  "Next Time, little bug," he muttered.
  "I promise! I am going to get you!"

Chapter 21

Maddy walked slowly and quietly.
She listened carefully for any sound.
There were no sounds in this drainpipe.

The drainpipe quickly climbed upwards.
Maddy climbed up with it.
This pipe wasn't smooth.
Raised ridges made climbing easier.

Two sharp curves in the pipe took away the light.
Now, she was climbing in the dark.

"I'm glad for these fine whiskers," Maddy thought.

In the pitch black dark, her whiskers showed her the way.
She passed another sharp curve.
Dim light trickled down from above.
Now, she could see.

At the sharp curve in the pipe, there was another pipe.
That pipe turned the other way. It traveled down into darkness.
That pipe looked dangerous.

"Just follow the light," Maddy reminded herself.

Up the drainpipe she went, almost to the top.
The last foot of the drainpipe went straight up.
She could see bricks where it opened at the top.
These were the bricks that built Gracie's front porch.
Maddy climbed up to the top of the drainpipe,
  and peeked over the edge.

In front,
  Magic's tail hung over the edge of the birdbath.
To one side,
  Gracie's flowers were being tickled by a honeybee.
To the other side,
  a garden green hose leaned up against the front porch.
And behind her,
  the round metal handle of a water spigot stuck out.
It attached the garden green hose to the front of Gracie's house.

"Mr. Bumbler," whispered Maddy.

"Sshhhhh," Bumbler whispered back.
He was hiding behind a brass flower pot,
  up on Gracie's front porch.

Maddy looked toward the "Sshhhhh" sound.
There, she saw Bumbler. He pointed to the bird bath.

Maddy nodded, then looked back to the front yard.
The black cat's tail moved along the edge of the bath.
It looked like a snake.

Maddy turned back toward Bumbler.
Bumbler waved a wing and a leg.
The coast was clear. Magic must be sleeping.

Maddy jumped out of the drainpipe.
She crawled across the coiled hose,
  then scrambled up to where it leaned against the bricks.
Jumping from the hose to the brick wall was easy.
Quickly and quietly, brick by brick, she pulled herself up.
She crawled over the top of the last brick,
  and tip-toed across Gracie's front porch.
Maddy made her way safely over to the brass flower pot.

  "Good to see you again," whispered Bumbler.
  "I was worried about you in that drainpipe."

  "It's good to see you too," she whispered back.

  "How are we going to get into the house?" asked Bumbler.

  "With this!" smiled Maddy as she held up her tiny gold key.
She tucked it into a small pocket on the back of her backpack.
  "Come, follow me."

Maddy ran quickly across the front porch.
A tall flowering trumpet vine hugged the corner post.
This vine climbed up and over and onto the roof.

Up the vine, Maddy climbed.
Buster Bumbler followed right behind.
Up to the top of the front porch roof, they went.
And there, hiding behind a big yellow trumpet flower,
  they looked out.

Bumbler looked up to the second story of the house.
There, he saw a balcony.
Up on the balcony were several fancy flower pots.
They rested safely behind a twisted metal railing.
Between Bumbler and the balcony were thick clay roof tiles.
These roof tiles looked steep and slippery.
And across the roof tiles climbed Gracie's trumpet vines.
These vines crawled all the way up to the top of the roof.
Most importantly..... there was no cat.

Maddy looked out from behind the trumpet flower.
What an amazing view!
She could see past Gracie's Garden.
But it was something else that caught her eye.
Something in Gracie's front yard.

"The bird bath is empty," whispered Maddy.

"Well, of course it's empty," Bumbler muttered back.
"The cat wouldn't be sleeping there if it were full."

"No, I mean it's empty!" said Maddy.
"There is no cat in the bird bath! Magic is gone!"

Bumbler turned around and looked down.

There was no cat in the empty bird bath.
So he looked around and across and up and everywhere.
There was no sign of the big black cat anywhere.

"How far away is the door?" asked Bumbler.

Maddy pointed up to the balcony.
   "It's behind those flower pots. See the fancy glass door?
     Next to it is another secret panel and another secret door."

"I will see if the coast is clear," said Bumbler.

He took off and buzzed away.
A few minutes later, he buzzed back.
   "I think it's safe for us to go," said Bumbler.
   "I don't see that cat anywhere."

"Follow me," Maddy whispered.

She ran up the hard, slippery, reddish-brown roof tiles,
   jumping over the trumpet vines in her way.
Bumbler followed her to the second floor balcony.
They hid behind the fancy flower pots.

"We made it," said Bumbler quietly.

Maddy took the little key out of the pocket.
She peeked out from behind the flower pots.
There was no cat on the balcony that she could see.

"Wait here until I open the door," said Maddy.

"No, I'm coming with you," objected Bumbler.
"I'm not afraid of any cat."

Maddy stepped out from behind the flower pots.
She ran to the edge of the fancy glass door.
Bumbler followed right behind.

Maddy pressed the small wood panel and pushed.
It opened just a little, then it stopped.
She pushed harder, but it was stuck.
As Maddy pushed against the wood panel,
  a dark shadow covered her from behind.

Maddy grabbed Bumbler,
  and pushed him into the small opening behind the secret panel.
  "Hide in here and be ready," she whispered.

  "Helllllloooo, little mouse," said a soft purring voice.
  "What are you doing out here all by yourself?"

Slowly, Maddy turned around.
The big black cat stood over her.

Maddy let Magic see the gold key in her hand.
Then slowly, she put both hands behind her back.
  "Just visiting," she answered.

The big black cat moved closer and sniffed the air.
  "Do you smell something delicious?" purred the cat.

  "Just the smell of Gracie's beautiful flowers." answered Maddy.

Maddy stepped back closer to the secret door,
  as the big black cat casually stretched out a paw.
  "You smell delicious, little mouse," purred the cat.
  "And it's almost lunchtime.
    You will make an excellent snack."

Maddy was trapped!
In front of her..... the big black cat.
Behind her..... the secret panel.
But the secret panel was stuck.
Maddy could not unlock the secret door.

With her hands behind her back,
  Maddy slipped the small key into her backpack.
Then, she slipped out something else.

  "Where were you hiding?" Maddy asked Magic.
  "I looked around up here. I did not see you.
    I didn't want to interrupt your day."

Magic purrrrred:
  "A tasty little mouse like YOU,
    could never interrupt my day.
  Little mice help a cat grow fat."

Magic thought about what he said for just a moment.
Then the cat's big black paw swiped through the air.
Long sharp claws reached out for Maddy.

Maddy pulled the sewing needle out from behind her back,
  and poked it deep into Magic Cat's paw.

85

"MEEE OWWWWWWWW!!!" screeched Magic.
Magic pulled away the paw in pain.

The needle pulled out of Magic's paw,
  and out of Maddy's hand.
It fell tinkling onto the balcony's hard tile floor.

"NOW, BUMBLER!!" yelled Maddy.

Bumbler buzzed out to help her.
  "Pick on somebody your own size!" he yelled.

Bumbler stabbed his sharp stinger at Magic,
  and jabbed it into the tip of the big black cat's nose.

"MEEE OWWWWWWWW!!!" Magic screeched again.
The big black cat was stung.

Maddy grabbed her sewing needle and ran.
She darted underneath Magic, jumped off the balcony,
  landed on the clay roof tiles and slid.

Down the slippery roof tiles, she slid, totally out of control.
Maddy scratched wildly for something to hold onto as
  she tumbled toward the edge.
She barely caught an arm of the trumpet vine.
Maddy held on to the vine as she slid off the roof.
The trumpet vine snapped away from the roof tiles,
  but the vine itself did not break.

"Whhhoooaaaaa!" yelled Maddy.

She squeezed the vine tightly in her tiny hands.
Holding on, she swooshed down through the air,
  and flew past the fancy front door of Gracie's house.
Then Maddy let go! She twirled through the air!
Landing gracefully on the front porch railing,
  she took a moment to catch her breath.
It felt good to be safe again.

She looked over the edge of the wood railing.
Down below was the black drainpipe.
All she had to do was climb down.

Bumbler flew through the air.
He wasn't far behind.
It was Bumbler who saw Magic first.

  "JUMP, Maddy!" he yelled, "JUMP!"

Magic leapt from a front porch post right toward Maddy.

There was no time to climb down. Maddy jumped!
Down toward the water spigot handle, she dropped.
Her tiny hands reached out for the handle and grabbed it.
But the handle turned.

Maddy grabbed for the handle over and over again.
She was trying not to fall.
As the handle turned, water sprayed everywhere.

  "MEEE OWWWWWWWW!!!" screeched Magic.
Cold water soaked the big black cat.

The water spigot handle stopped turning.
But the wild spray of water did not.
Water flooded around the drainpipe.

Maddy held on as best she could.
Below her, a wild whirlpool of water twisted and turned.
Bumbler flew bravely to the little mouse.
  "Try to hold on to me!" he yelled.

But the water was too much. Maddy's hands slipped,
  and Bumbler's wings were hit by the spray.

As Maddy fell, she reached out and grabbed him.
She pulled Bumbler close and held him tight.
They splashed down into the whirlpool below,
  where the cold harsh water pulled them under.
They swirled three times around,
  then the water pulled them down.
Down into the drainpipe, they went.

  "HOLD ON!!!" cried Maddy.

The rushing water pulled them.
They bounced to the left.
They should have gone right.

Maddy and Buster Bumbler were forced down into the darkness.
There was no light when they rushed past the next curve.
The water was dragging them deep underground,
  and there was nothing they could do.
Drainpipes are dangerous.

Chapter 22

Zacky stood tall and confident.
The Great Glowworm Meeting Hall was built for Kings.
But that did not intimidate Zacky.
After all..... they were bugs..... just like him.

"I stand before the Firefly Council with special purpose.
  Gracie's Garden, our home, is under attack.
  An army of Garden Snails is invading our homeland.
  They are destroying the lower gardens as we speak.
  I am here today to ask the lightning bugs to join with us,
     and work together for the good of the garden.
  I am here today asking for an alliance."

Several members of the council gasped.
Lightning bugs began speaking out of turn.

One council member said,
  "Not Possible! There can be no alliance!"

89

"I wouldn't join forces with a CODE TRAITOR!" said another.

An old grumpy firefly said,
"No respectable lightning bug would hear of such a thing!"

"Just the idea is a slap in the face!" said a short, plump firefly.

In the corner of the hall stood the firefly guards.
Colonel Lampy stood in front of them.
He was the most powerful lightning bug in the garden.

"Quiet down, Council!" demanded Colonel Lampy.

Queen Maggie's soft, gentle voice spoke with authority,
"Let us hear what the Code Cricket has to say."

Zacky spoke calmly.
"YES, I am a Code Cricket,
    just as my father was before me.
Many years ago the fireflies and crickets were friends.
We worked together to make life better for all living creatures.
Codes using light and sound were mixed together.
These codes helped us talk to one another.
Together, as friends, we shared that power.
Then that friendship was torn apart."

"Queen Maggie, your father and my father were selfish.
Power and control were more important than friendship.
Their selfish ways broke the peace between us.
The pride of our fathers has been our downfall."

"Yes, Code Cricket, I agree with you," replied Queen Maggie.
"Mistakes were made on both sides.
We were stronger when we worked together.
I have discussed an alliance with the council."

For a moment, Zacky looked hopeful.

Queen Maggie continued.
"The council majority will vote against an alliance.
The glowworm species no longer has any trust in others.
The lightning bugs have decided to work alone."

Zacky thought they were making a big mistake.
He looked at each one of the council members.
Each of them looked away.
Maybe they were ashamed.
Or maybe they were trying to hide something.

Zacky turned away from the council and walked a few steps.
Without looking back, he spoke to them.
"The animals of Gracie's Garden should be working together.
Let me know when you have changed your minds."

Zacky made several strange cricket noises.
High pitched musical notes rang throughout the hall.
He listened to the sound waves as they echoed back.
Then, Zacky left.

Chapter 23

"Seeeeee Yaaaaa," giggled Roley as he flew through the air.
He landed in Maddy's ladybug water fountain,
  and laughed as the water dripped off of him.

"Wouldn't want to Beeee Yaaa!"

Bailey perched on Maddy's front porch.
  "It's always good to see you splash back," she said.
  "Are you talking to yourself again?"

Roley smiled, "Nope!
  Just re-living some great memories.
  Where's Zacky?"

  "I don't know," answered Bailey. "It's already seven-thirty.
  He was supposed to meet me here at seven."

"It's not like him to be late," said Roley.

"There are lots of things not right," said Bailey.
"Did you see the Garden Snails in the lower garden?
  I could see over a hundred from the air."

"I saw them from The Edge," replied Roley.
"There are probably a thousand of them.
  They are eating and destroying the plants from underneath.
  A Grove Snail is telling them what to do."

"A Grove snail?" asked Bailey.

"Yep," said Roley, "that's what he said.
  He calls himself General Nemoralis.
  He's a big bossy snail, full of meanness.
  This army of snails is not good."

Zacky's voice fell from the roof of Maddy's country house.
  "No, it's not good. It's definitely..... not good."

"Where have you been?" Roley and Bailey asked.
They watched Zacky climb down quickly and quietly.

"Sorry, I'm late," said Zacky.
"I went to speak to the Firefly Council."

"Fireflies do not like to talk," said Bailey.
"Though, sometimes they will talk with me."

"They don't talk to roley poleys," said Roley Roanin.
"They just blink their lights,
    and expect everyone to know what they're thinking."

Roley whirled around. "Zacky, did they speak with you?"

"Yes, I spoke with the Firefly Council," answered Zacky.

"Will they fight against the snails?" asked Bailey.
"Will they work with us to protect Gracie's Garden?"

"No, they refuse to make an alliance," answered Zacky.

"Well, what are they going to do?" asked Roley Roanin.

"They will protect their homes," said Zacky,
    "and protect the nectar and pollen they eat.
  But they will not work with us to defend Gracie's Garden."

"Sounds kind of foolish if you ask me," said Roley.
"We would be stronger if we worked together."

"Unless," mumbled Zacky.

"Unless what?" asked Bailey.

"Unless the Firefly Council wants something more," said Zacky.
"They may want more than just to defend themselves."

"Like what?" asked Roley.

"Maybe they want to control the snails," answered Zacky.
"Then the lightning bugs can feed their glowworm armies.
  More glowworms mean more power and more lightning bugs.
  They might be able to take control of Gracie's Garden."

"Gracie's Garden is for all of us," said Roley.
"Would those flashing, flying beetle buggers really do that?"

"I'm not sure," answered Zacky.
"But I did discover something else.
  The lightning bugs have a secret."

"And what is that?" asked Bailey.

"They are hiding something," whispered Zacky,
  "in a chamber of the Great Glowworm Meeting Hall,
    and protecting it very carefully.
  I believe it's some sort of weapon."

"How can we know for sure?" asked Roley Roanin.

"Two good friends of mine could help me find out," said Zacky.
"How would you like to play a dangerous little game?
  I like to call it 'I Spy on a Firefly'!"

"Sounds like a lot of fun to me!" said Roley.
"Count me in, too," said Bailey, "I want to play."

"Let's get going," said Zacky.

Off to the Great Glowworm Meeting Hall, they traveled together.
They would visit the lightning bugs in the middle of the night.
Above them, the big round moon already hung in the sky.

"This is going to be fun!" smiled Roley.
"This is going to be fun!"

Chapter 24

Down, Down, Down they went,
  wild water rushing all around them.
Past one curve and then another,
  Maddy and Bumbler were spinning out of control.

Then the drainpipe ended and spit them out.
They splashed down over a rumbling waterfall,
  and into a larger drainpipe.
There, the falling water forced them under.

Maddy paddled frantically in the rough and tumbling water.
She raised herself and Bumbler up to the surface.
The water pushed them up against the wall of the pipe.
To their left, the rough river tried to pull them away.
To their right, this new drainpipe climbed up.
Going up was their only chance.

Maddy gasped for air.

"Hold on to me, Bumbler!" she sputtered.

She struggled as the river tried to pull Bumbler away.
She almost lost him..... but she didn't.

Maddy held Bumbler up and with all her strength, she jumped.
They landed half in and half out of the wild river.
Above her, the ridges of the pipe were dry!
She lifted Bumbler up over the ridges,
  and pushed him to higher ground.
He was out of the water and safe.

Then Maddy struggled to pull herself up.
She was almost over that slippery wet ridge,
  when a wild wave grabbed her.
The rough and tumbling water dragged her away.

Maddy tumbled too.
Over and over and over she turned,
  knocking against the bumpy floor of the drainpipe.

Then suddenly, she stopped.
A crack in the drainpipe caught the strap of her backpack.
The raging river pulled her to the bottom.
She fought against the wild water,
  but there was nothing she could do.

Maddy struggled and struggled and struggled.
Cold water in the pitch black drainpipe swallowed her up.
The world around Maddy M. Mouse disappeared.
Drainpipes..... are dangerous.

Chapter 25

"Shhhh," Zacky shushed Roley Roanin.

"I can't help it," Roley muttered back.
"This stump is all rotted. The bark just keeps falling off."

"Try to be just a little bit quieter," hushed Zacky.
"Come on, let's keep moving."

Together they climbed up the rotting old tree stump.
Over the black weathered bark, they went.
Then Zacky stopped.

"Be careful little sea creature," he warned.
"Just ahead is a really rotten place."

Roley climbed up next to Zacky.
"Stop worrying about me," mumbled Roley.
"I live in a rotten hollow log."

"Just be careful," said Zacky.

"How much farther to the secret passage?" asked Roley.

"Just a little further," answered Zacky.
"We'll be there in no time.
  On the other side of this bark is a steep wall.
  We have to climb that wall up to a small ledge.
  Above the ledge is a small cave.
  That cave hides the entrance to the secret tunnel,
    and that secret tunnel will take us right inside."

They both peeked out from behind a big piece of rotting bark.

  "She's just on time," whispered Zacky.
  "Bailey is going to distract them."

Bailey fluttered down softly.
She began talking with the firefly guards.

  "Anyone will talk to that pretty little butterfly," smiled Roley.

  "Bailey will keep them busy," said Zacky.
  "But those guards will be right below us.
    We have to be very quiet. Come on, let's go."

Zacky and Roley crawled silently over the thick bark,
  then slowly up the stump's steep wall.
Here, they were directly above Bailey and the guards.
And below them, the two firefly guards were chatting away.

The lightning bug guards were distracted.
They were very busy talking,
  talking with a pretty little butterfly.

Zacky and Roley Roanin scrambled over the ledge.
Up and over and into the cave, Roley rolled.
He knocked his head on something hard.

  "Oww!" moaned Roley, "This is a dead end!"
  "There is some kind of round metal door."

  "Yes, there is a door," said Zacky.

Roley rubbed the top of his head.
  "That's what I just said. There's a door!"

Roley stood up and turned to face Zacky.
  "You told me there was a ledge," he whispered.
  "You told me there was a little cave.
    And you told me there was a secret tunnel.
    You never said anything about a door!"

  "It's right in front of you, Roley," Zacky whispered back.
  "And it's quite obviously a door.
    It's too heavy for lightning bugs to open.
    That's why they don't use this tunnel anymore.
    And that's why it's called a secret tunnel."

  "You should have told me about the door," grumbled Roley.

Zacky moved past Roley to the big, round, metal door.

"As a matter of fact," said Zacky,
  "this door is too heavy for almost any bug.
  But it's not too heavy for the legs of a jumping cricket."

Zacky opened it.
The round metal door swiveled,
  and behind it, there really was a secret tunnel.
Dim, soft, golden-yellow light spilled out.
It glimmered across the shiny, round, hard, brown metal door.

This strange metal door captivated Roley.
On the one side, there were odd shaped lines and curves.
Half of the face of a man with a beard was carved on the other.

  "This door is made with a penny," said Zacky.
  "Gracie put it here. That's what she called it."
Zacky squeezed through the opening.

Roley Roanin rubbed his little hands across the penny.
He liked it.
  "I need to get one of these for my log," he smiled.
Then he followed Zacky.

They scuttled through the dusty, neglected tunnel.
As they moved forward, the light grew brighter.
The secret tunnel led them to the center of the rotten stump.
Roley and Zacky crawled out onto an abandoned balcony.
Broken stick railings and bug garbage lay everywhere.
Trash cluttered the balcony.

  "What a mess," muttered Roley.

Zacky and Roley crawled to the edge of the balcony.
They watched their steps, careful not to make any noise.
They were high above the Great Glowworm Meeting Hall.
Fireflies in the great hall below were talking.

The two friends tip-toed down an old stairway.
Zacky stopped in the middle and pointed to the fireflies.
He put a finger up to his lips to say "shhhh",
  but he didn't make a sound.

They crept quietly down to the next balcony.
This one was clean and neat.
Zacky waved for Roley to follow him closely.
They crossed the balcony, staying close to the edge.
There, they heard two lightning bugs talking.

Zacky and Roley listened.
Roley smiled and almost giggled.
It was fun to be spying on these bugs.

The first voice they heard was soft and gentle.
  "When will you attack the snails?"

  "That is up to Colonel Lampy," said another lightning bug.
This bug had a deep, gruff voice.

  "Do we have enough soldiers?" asked the softer voice.
  "Is the glowworm army ready to fight?"

  "Colonel Lampy will make that decision," said the gruff voice.
  "He is in charge of the glowworm army."

"But we have to have enough soldiers," said the other.
"And they have to be ready to fight."

The gruff voice responded sharply.
  "Colonel Lampy has a secret weapon.
    He will make the Garden Snails surrender.
    They will be food for the glowworms!
    Those tasty snails will help us grow our glowworm armies.
    More glowworms means more lightning bugs.
    No one will be able to stop us!"

  "What will you do about Queen Maggie?" asked the soft voice.
  "She is demanding an alliance with the garden animals.
    She is trying to convince the council to join with Zacky."

The gruff voice replied gruffly.
  "Colonel Lampy controls the power of the glowworm army.
    Colonel Lampy is the strongest and smartest Firefly alive.
    Queen Maggie is a new Queen. She has no real power!
    As we speak, Colonel Lampy is having her locked away."

  "Locked away!" gasped the soft voice.
  "But she's the Queen!"

  "Not for long," snapped the gruff voice.
  "Colonel Lampy is taking control of everything.
    Soon he will be King of the Fireflies.
    Then, he will squash Queen Maggie like a bug."

Zacky and Roley moved forward.
They had heard enough.

They continued across the balcony,
  and climbed down through a different tunnel.
Turning a corner into a quiet hallway, they stopped.

  "Did you know," asked Roley,
    "that the lightning bugs are not working together?"

  "I suspected there was trouble," answered Zacky.
  "But I didn't suspect Queen Maggie was in so much danger."

  "And it sounds like the Queen wants an alliance," said Roley.
  "The Queen wants us all to work together to protect the garden.
    This Colonel Lamp-Head has got to be stopped!"

  "I agree," said Zacky.
  "This Colonel Lampy is dangerous.
    And we will need to help Queen Maggie.
    Follow me."

Zacky crawled quickly down the tunnel.
Roley Roanin followed after him.
They came to yet another tunnel.
It sloped down into the tree stump.

  "Where are we going now?" asked Roley.

Zacky turned and smiled.
  "To find ourselves a secret weapon!"

Chapter 26

"Why am I a prisoner?
   Why won't you answer me?
   Are you going to feed me to the glowworms?
   Can I talk to somebody in charge?
   Do you have anything to eat?"

Sammy asked these questions over and over again.
But no one answered him. The guards were silent.
He was tired of being all tied up and hungry.

"Do you have any Garden Snail eggs?" he asked.
"I love to eat Garden Snail eggs!"

Nothing had changed.
He was stuck in a room with no doors and no windows.
Nobody in charge came to tell him anything.
And he was still all tied up and hungry.
Nothing had changed.

Suddenly, the room darkened.
The light from the center of the ceiling faded.
And there, in the center of the ceiling, was a hole.

"The Colonel must be coming!" said the little guard.
"Stand up straight and be ready."

The big guard replied,
"Maybe we'll get to see the beautiful Queen?"

The little guard sneered.
"You fool! She doesn't know the prisoner is here!
The Queen thinks her Royal Guards have the prisoner.
I told you we are working for Colonel Lampy.
Only Colonel Lampy!"

The big guard looked confused.
"But isn't the Queen in charge of Colonel Lampy?"

"Not for long," said the little guard.
"Now be quiet and stand at attention.
You don't want to upset Colonel Lampy.
Soon he will be our new King!
Stand up straight and don't let your backside shine!
Colonel Lampy likes to show off his own."

Then the light in the center of the ceiling went out.
The room went completely black and silent.

"Colonel Lampy, is that you?" asked the little guard.

The little guard looked up at the center of the ceiling.
He slowly stretched, turned his backside up,
  and glowed.

It was the strangest sight Sammy ever saw.
In the middle of the ceiling, there was the hole.
Sticking out of that hole was a silly looking ball of gray scales.
And below this ball of gray scales was the body of a cricket.

  "NOW!!" shouted Zacky.

He tossed the curled up Roley Roanin into the room.
Roley hit the little guard right in the chest.
Zacky climbed down quickly after him.

Zacky grabbed the big guard,
  and held him up against the wall.
He used just one of his strong back legs.
Then Zacky picked up the little guard.
With three of his strong front legs,
  he held the little guard up in the air.

Sammy was surprised.
He watched it all happen in just a second's time.

Roley Roanin rolled twice around the room,
  making sure nobody else was there.
He stopped right in front of Sammy.

  "HEY little FELLA!" smiled Roley.
  "Good to see you again!"

Still smiling, Roley Roanin plucked one of the ropes.
   "These sure are tight. This can't be good for your posture."

   "Cut him loose, Roley," said Zacky.

   "Yes, SIR, General Grasshopper."

Roley curled up and whizzed around the little snail.
Roley held out the edge of his sharp crustacean shell.
Three times around and the ropes were cut to shreds.

   "Those ropes are the perfect size," said Zacky.
   "Wouldn't you agree, my little sea creature?"

Roley Roanin whipped around the guards.
Roley, the ropes, and the guards were a blur.
When he stopped, both guards were tied up tight.

Zacky stood back and looked at the guards.
The little guard was obviously angry and frustrated.
The big guard looked a little scared.

   "Colonel Lampy is going to get you for this!" said the little one.

   "Maybe," said Zacky calmly, "and maybe not.
      Now, I have a few questions for you."

   "I have nothing to say to a Cricket!" snapped the little guard.

   "And how about you big fella?"
Zacky asked the big guard nicely.

The big guard's voice was nervous and shaky.
  "They don't really tell me anything," he replied.
  "The little guard just told me about Queen Maggie.
    I was only guarding the prisoner."

  "Told you what?" asked Zacky.
  "Told you what?"

The big guard answered honestly.
  "Colonel Lampy is working against the Queen.
    Colonel Lampy is going to make himself King."

  "You better keep your mouth shut!" snarled the little guard.
  "I'm going to tell Colonel Lampy about this!"

Roley Roanin spoke up,
  "Hey, I'll tell you what you can tell Colonel Lamp-Head.
    Tell him there are no prisoners here in Gracie's Garden!"

Zacky picked up Sammy.
He lifted him up to the light in the ceiling.
Sammy pulled himself into the light.
Through the light and into the tunnel, he slid.
He was happy to be untied and free.

Roley Roanin shrunk into a ball.
He rolled three times around the little room.
With super speed, he rolled right up the wall,
  crossed the ceiling to the center,
  grabbed the edge of the hole,
  and hung upside down.

Golden light sparkled around Roley's hard crustacean shell.
He smiled down at the guards and waved.
  "SEE Ya.....WOULDN't Want to BEE Ya!"
Then Roley Roanin rolled up into the tunnel,
  and followed after Sammy.

Zacky reached over to the big guard and untied him.
  "Big Guard," said Zacky.
  "I am untying you so that you can do the right thing.
    Warn Queen Maggie of their plans.
    Help her."

Zacky turned silent. He was thinking again.
Pictures of Gracie's Garden danced in his head.
He pictured the Garden Center and the garden green hose.
He saw Gracie's blue wheelbarrow standing quiet and still.
This wheelbarrow held her garden tools up off the ground.
And it held Gracie's watering can..... tall, pink and round.

Zacky caught an idea.
Then he whispered into Big Guard's ear.
Zacky whispered three important things.

Then, with his strong back legs, he grabbed the edge of the
  ceiling tunnel and pulled himself up into the hole.
Zacky stuck his head back out.
  "Have a good day gentlemen," he smiled.
  "It has been a pleasure to meet you!"

Zacky winked and then he waved and then he turned,
  and crawled away.

Chapter 27

Buster Bumbler was all out of buzz,
  and dazed from the rough ride down the drainpipe.
Maddy had been next to him just minutes ago.
She had saved his life when he was supposed to be saving hers.
And now, Maddy was gone.

  "I can not fail my friends," moaned Buster Bumbler.
  "I will not fail. I will not fail. I will not fail."
He said this to himself over and over again.

Bumbler shook himself and struggled to get up.
He looked down the drainpipe.
The rushing water was gone.
Except for the occasional sound of a water drop dripping,
  all was quiet.

Behind him, soft light crept down the cross pipe.
In front of him, the cross pipe traveled down into darkness.

Bumbler shook his wet wings. There was no buzz.
Climbing down the pipe was his only chance of finding Maddy.
So, he pulled himself up over the ridge and tumbled down.
Up the next ridge, he tumbled down again.

Over and over he tumbled down the pipe hoping to find her,
  hoping she was alright.

  "Maddy M," Bumbler called out.
  "Maddy M..... I'm coming."

Bumbler tumbled down the next ridge and hit something.
It was the strap of Maddy's backpack.
And there, next to him, in a small pool of water lay Maddy.
She wasn't moving.

Bumbler unhooked the strap and pulled away the backpack.
He lifted her chin and listened closely.
She was not breathing.

  "Maddy!" he said loudly.
Buster Bumbler shook her.
  "Maddy!"
She did not move.

Buster Bumbler shook his wings again.
Now they were buzzing. They lifted him up.
He lifted up and over her.
Buzzing above her heart, he dropped.
He landed like a rock.
Water gushed out of Maddy's mouth.

Three more times Buster Bumbler buzzed up into the air.
And three more times he landed like a rock.
He was thumping the water out of her.

Maddy coughed and gasped for air.
She was cold and shaking..... shaking uncontrollably.

Buster Bumbler held her and whispered,
  "I apologize for what I have to do next."

Bumbler wiped the water off the end of his stinger.
With no hesitation, he gave Maddy a shot.
A stinging shot right in the arm.

  "One millisecond of venom should be enough," he said,
    "enough for a soldier your size."

Maddy felt a warm burning sensation in her arm.
As the venom spread through her, the shaking stopped.
She turned herself over and coughed some more.

  "Bumbler," Maddy said quietly.
  "I do believe you have just saved my life."

Buster Bumbler smiled.
  "Just doing my job, ma'am."

  "How far down the pipe did I go?" she asked.

  "Not too far," he answered.
  "You were saved by the strap on your backpack."

Maddy rubbed her sore arm. "Thanks for the shot..... I think?"

"We need to get out of this pipe," said Bumbler.
"Can you move?"

"I'm stiff and sore, but I'm not dead!" answered Maddy.
"Let's get going."

Maddy checked her backpack,
  and swung it over her good shoulder.

"Bumbler," she said, "climb up onto my backpack.
  I'm strong enough to carry you.
  It will not be easy to fly in this pipe."

"I can fly anywhere," said Bumbler.
"I would never be a burden to you or any soldier."

Up the drainpipe, they went.
It was dark, this drainpipe, but not pitch black.
Soft light reached down to them.

Soon, they came to where the drainpipes crossed.
  "That's the way we came down," said Bumbler.
  He pointed up to the pipe, the one that spit them out.

But Maddy had already passed him by.
  "The light is coming from up here," she called back.
  "Let's try following the light."

Maddy climbed the ridges. Buster Bumbler followed after her.

The flying Bumbler kept bumping his head on the ceiling.

"Flying in a drainpipe is not easy," mumbled Bumbler.

"It doesn't look easy," said Maddy.

Bumbler buzzed back into the ceiling again.
His wings sputtered as he bumped his head.

"It doesn't sound easy either," Maddy chuckled.
"I did offer to let you hang on to my backpack."

Bumbler responded seriously,
  "I would never weigh a soldier down!"

Up the pipe they went, following the light.
Then the pipe curved sharply. It curved straight up.
Maddy and Bumbler looked up.
Lines of light glared down.
This was the end of the drainpipe!

But, at the very end of the pipe was a cap of metal bars.
These metal bars blocked the way out.

"I believe I'm small enough," said Bumbler.
"I can squeeze through those bars."

Bumbler buzzed, bouncing his way up the pipe.
Then he wiggled through the bars and into a small room.
There, on the wall, a lightbulb stuck out.
This lightbulb lit up the room.

He buzzed around and looked around,
  then landed on the metal bars looking down.

  "It's a room!" Bumbler called down to Maddy.
  "It's a room in the house!"

Maddy climbed up after him.
She climbed the last few inches of the pipe,
  and pushed against the metal bars.
The bars lifted up a little,
  just enough for her to squeeze through.

Maddy climbed out of the drainpipe,
  then pushed the cap of metal bars back down.

Maddy stood up, looked around the room and smiled.
  "Bumbler! We are in the basement!
   This is the inside of Gracie's house!
   Now all we have to do is find her."

Chapter 28

Roley Roanin rolled after Sammy.
The short tunnel led them to another room.
Roley uncurled himself and made a yucky face,
  as he wiped snail slime from his scales.

"Why do snails have all this disgusting slime?" asked Roley.

"It helps us stick to the job," chuckled Sammy.
"We can climb straight up and upside down.
  Our sticky slime is slippery, too.
  It lets us stick and slide all at the same time.
  It's really great stuff."

"If you're a snail!" grumbled Roley Roanin.

Roley pointed to another tunnel.
  "We have got to keep moving."

119

Sammy slid towards the tunnel.

"Wait a second, Slimy!" said Roley.

"My name is Sammy," said the little snail.

"Yeah, I know that, but I have something important to say."
Roley talked as he walked towards the tunnel.

"And what is that?" asked Sammy.

"I'm going first!" yelled Roley as he jumped in front of Sammy.
"I'm not going to get slimed the whole way out of here."

Roley Roanin rolled forward into the next tunnel.
He laughed as he led the way.
Sammy followed.

It was hard for Roley Roanin to go slowly,
  but he did it anyway.
He stopped and waited quietly where tunnels crossed,
  looked carefully for guards at every turn,
  and led Sammy through the tunnels to the balcony.
Below, in the great meeting hall, they heard voices.

"Sshhh," whispered Roley, "follow me."

They crossed the first balcony quietly and headed up the stairs.
Roley moved trash and debris out of Sammy's way.
Everything was going just as planned.
Soon Sammy would be free.

"RUN! ROLEY! RUN!"

Zacky yelled up to them from the lower balcony.

Roley and Sammy looked down.
Big, noisy firefly guards swarmed through the tunnel.
Punching, kicking, chopping, and slicing through the air,
  Zacky held them back.

  "Light the alarm! Light the alarm!" yelled the guards.

Roley Roanin pulled Sammy up the last stair.
They made their way to the middle of the upper balcony.

  "That Way!" shouted Roley.
He pointed Sammy in the direction of the escape tunnel,
  then rolled up onto the ledge of the rotting wood balcony.

Firefly guards flew up from the great hall below.
Zacky climbed backwards up the stairs to the second balcony.
He was fighting to hold back the lightning bugs,
  and slowly retreating up the stairway.
He knocked several guards over the wall.

  "Get Sammy into the tunnel," yelled Zacky.

More Firefly guards landed on the ledge of the balcony.
These guards saw Sammy and rushed to get him.

But, Roley Roanin distracted them.
  "Here I Am! Over Here!" he yelled.

Waving his arms and legs, Roley ran right towards them.
And just before he reached the guards, he curled up.
The little ball of energy smashed right through them.
Ping! Ping! Ping-Ping-Ping!

The five guards, knocked upside down, fell back over the wall.

"More fun than bowling!" shouted Roley Roanin.

"Stop playing games, little sea creature!" yelled Zacky.
"Help me!"

Zacky reached the top of the stairs.
More guards were trying to push their way through.
Zacky was fighting harder than ever.

Roley Roanin stretched out, looking quite relaxed.
"Zacky, it looks like you've got them under control."

Firefly guards dropped out of the air onto the balcony.
They moved toward the opening of the escape tunnel.

Roley Roanin rolled up again.
"Give me a kick, Zacky!"

"There's nothing I'd rather do right now!" Zacky yelled back.

Zacky kicked the rolled up roley poley.
It was really just a hard shove with his strong back leg.
Roley Roanin whizzed across the upper balcony.

POP! POP! POP! POP! POP! POP! POP! POP!

All the guards on the balcony were knocked to the floor.
Roley rolled to the opening of the escape tunnel.
He looked inside. Sammy was almost to the secret door.

"Sammy, Go as Fast as you Can!" shouted Roley.

"Take the high road on your way out!" Sammy shouted back.

"What?" asked Roley.

"Travel on the ceiling," shouted Sammy.
"I have a surprise for our friendly fireflies."
Sammy turned and continued to slide.

Zacky fought with all his legs.
"ROLEY!" he huffed.
"Do you think you could help out an old friend?
You have fourteen legs!"

Roley Roanin leaned casually up against the wall.
"Well, it looks to me like you are doing a fine job."

Zacky struggled to keep the guards back.

Roley Roanin continued to talk.
"I've heard of Ninja Turtles before,
but never a Ninja Cricket.
Zacky, where did you learn all those fancy moves?"

More firefly guards swarmed to attack Zacky.
They attacked from every direction.
  "Roley," huffed Zacky,
  "I don't really..... have the time to..... talk about that.....
    just now..... but maybe we can sit down..... and.....
    tell old stories..... around the campfire..... sometime."

  "Sure, Zacky, that sounds nice," smiled Roley.

Roley glanced into the secret tunnel, then calmly turned back.
  "Zacky, if you're done playing games, I think it's time to go.
    Our friend Sammy is at the end of the tunnel."

Zacky knocked back six guards at one time.
He calmly turned to Roley and smiled.
  "Sounds like a good idea, little sea creature!"

Then Zacky turned back and continued fighting like a wild bug.

  "Can you lend me another little boost of energy?" asked Roley.
  "Sammy told us to stick to the ceiling on our way out of here."

  "I'll be glad to kick you anytime!" said Zacky.
He knocked over seven or eight more guards.
Then Zacky tightened up his back leg
  and pushed Roley into the tunnel.

Roley Roanin was gone in a blur.
He traveled on the ceiling of the tunnel.
He made it all the way to the copper penny door.

Zacky backed up into the tunnel.
He fought the guards with one hand.
With the other, he pulled out a rotted board.
The ceiling of the tunnel collapsed.
Rubble blocked the firefly guards.

While they worked to clear it away,
  Zacky had time to turn and run.
He moved swiftly across the ceiling of the secret tunnel.
Zacky was an expert at crawling upside down.
Halfway to the penny door, he heard the guards break through.
The little cricket sped forward.

When Zacky came through the door, Roley giggled.
Snail slime covered the top of Zacky's head.

  "I told you to take the ceiling," laughed Roley.

  "I did," said Zacky, "but I'm taller than you."

Zacky pushed on the copper penny door.

Roley started laughing again.
He pointed to the guards in the tunnel.
  "It doesn't look like the firefly guards were so lucky."

Zacky, Roley and Sammy looked into the tunnel together.
The guards were stopped and struggling.
They were stuck in puddles of snail slime.

  "Good job, Slimy!" cheered Roley.

Zacky closed the door.
There, on the ledge waiting for them, was Bailey.
She was beautiful in the moonlight.

Her sweet voice greeted Sammy.
  "Hello, little Decollate snail. Good to see you again!"

Sammy blushed and smiled back, "Nice to see you, too!"

Zacky looked over the ledge.
  "We have to get out of here before the guards come."

Bailey looked at Roley Roanin.
  "Are you ready?" she asked.

Roley Roanin curled up tight and rolled over to Bailey.
He stuck out his little head and looked at Zacky and Sammy.
  "The thought of flying gives me the creeps," he muttered.

Then Bailey grabbed him with her little legs,
 and lifted up into the air.

  "Go Slow, Bailey!" hollered Roley.

But Bailey took off quickly, disappearing into the night.
Sammy and Zacky could hear them clearly.

Roley Roanin was screaming,
  "I Said Slow! I Said Slow!"
And Bailey was laughing,
  "This Is Slow! This Is Slow!"

"HALT! STOP! DON'T MOVE!"

The guards shouted at them from the top of the tree stump.
Almost a hundred guards were up above.
Zacky saw them in the moonlight.

Zacky turned to Sammy, "Are you ready to go?"

"There's no way I can outrun them," sighed Sammy.
"Just go without me."

"No need to outrun them, if you can trust me," said Zacky.

Sammy looked up.
The firefly guards were getting closer.
"You've helped me to escape once already," he said.
"Zacky, I do trust you."

Zacky grabbed Sammy with his front legs.
He hopped over to the ledge.

"I've got you, little fella!" said Zacky.
"Don't Worry."
Zacky bent his strong back legs to the ground.
The guards were close, but not close enough.
Zacky pushed off with all his strength and shot up into the air.

"Yipppeee!!" yelled Sammy.

They climbed up and up and up and up.
They jumped high over the plants of Gracie's Garden.

For a moment they stopped in the air,
  weightless and floating.
Sammy could see the garden lit by the moon,
  an amazing sight he never expected to see.

Then gravity pulled them down.
Sammy looked at the tall plants below.
Sammy's tummy rolled as they fell faster and faster.
There was no way his shell would protect him from this fall.
Sammy wanted to scream, but nothing came out.

Almost at the tops of the tallest plants,
  Zacky's back legs held Sammy tighter.

  "POOFFFFF!!"

This shuddering sound shook Sammy's shell.
It was the sound of Zacky's wings.
They swooped above the tops of the garden plants.
Air rushed past them with the great speed of flying.

  "Yipppeee!!" yelled Sammy again.

Zacky smiled as they flicked through the air.
  "We'll be there soon, little fella," chirped Zacky.
  "We'll be there soon."

Chapter 29

"Come, follow me," said Maddy.

Maddy scurried across the floor.
She wiggled under a door.
Then, as fast as lightning, she ran.

She scampered across cold hard tiles,
  then crossed the thick golden carpet.
Around a corner and down a hallway she flew.
Buster Bumbler followed right behind.

At the end of the hallway were stairs.
The thick carpet made climbing easy.
But flying was faster. Bumbler passed her up.

At the top of the stairs, Maddy stopped.
Buster Bumbler was already there,
  trying to crawl underneath the door.

But something blocked his way.
Bumbler kept searching.

"I found it!" he buzzed with excitement.

"What did you find?" asked Maddy.

"A small opening," he answered.
"Something is blocking the bottom of this door.
  But here, in the corner, I can see through."
Buster Bumbler wiggled through the hole.

Maddy crawled to the corner.
"I think I can squeeze through too," she said.

Maddy grabbed the edge of the black rubber barrier.
It was blocking her way under the door.
She pulled and it moved a little.
It moved on a metal track.

The hole was bigger now,
  just big enough for her to wiggle through.

Maddy ran across the slippery wood floor,
  turned, and ran down another hallway.
Buster Bumbler buzzed above her.
This hallway led to a large open area.

"Gracie calls this the foyer," said Maddy.
"Fancy people come through that door for parties."

Bumbler looked up at the fancy front door.
Polished glass windows were lined with copper edges.
Thick dark wood held the many pieces of carved glass together.
Above the fancy front door, windows stretched up two stories.
To the side, was a grand set of marble stairs.
This grand stairway curved upwards to the second floor.

"How are you going to climb these stairs?" Bumbler asked.
"They are tall and slippery. There is no carpet."

"I'm not," answered Maddy.

She walked around the stairway.
Behind the curve of the great stairway were windows.
The tall windows reached up two stories, overlooked the stairs,
  and were decorated with drapes.
Maddy pointed to where the drapes climbed up.

"I am going to climb these drapes," said Maddy.
"The drapes will bring me close to the stairs over there.
  It's a good thing I keep myself in tip-top shape."

Hand over hand she pulled herself up.
She climbed the drapes until she was more than half way.
Here, the drapes almost touched the stairway's banister.
The fancy wood railing was just inches away.

Maddy held on to the drapes with one hand,
  and started swinging her little body.
She counted the swings,
  "ONE! TWO! THREE!"

On the last swing, she let go.
She turned and twisted through the air,
  falling right towards the fancy wood banister.

Maddy landed perfectly..... but then..... she slid.
She slid down the perfectly polished wood railing.
Her sharp little claws almost didn't stop her,
  but they did.

Buster Bumbler buzzed up next to the little mouse.
  "Are you sliding just for fun?" he asked.

Maddy gave Bumbler a serious look.
  "I did not plan on sliding at all!" she said.
  "I was planning to climb this banister all the way to the top.
   It's a bit more slippery than I thought it would be.
   I may have to find another way."

Maddy tried to climb up the banister.
She pulled herself up one inch, then slid down two.
The polished wood railing was just too slippery.

She looked over the edge and smiled.
Wooden posts held up the railing.
There were two posts on every stair.
These posts gave Maddy an idea.

She swung herself over the edge of the banister,
  grabbed onto one of the fancy wood posts,
  and slid down the post like a fireman.

On her way down, she jumped to the next stair going up.
Then she climbed up the next post and jumped to the next stair.
Post after post and stair after stair, she made her way to the top.

At the top of the stairs, Maddy ran down another hallway.
Buster Bumbler buzzed right above her the entire way.
Then she stopped in front of a pink and yellow door.

Maddy wiggled under.
Bumbler followed.

They entered the prettiest little room there ever was.
Light gentle country colors danced across the walls.
There were soft pinks, quiet yellows and a touch of baby blue.
Gracie's bedroom window brightened up the room.

In one corner was a shelf for books.
In another corner..... a box for toys.

Along the biggest wall rested Gracie's big white bed.
It was covered with an elegant canopy of pretty white lace.
On the wall, beside the window, hung a fancy antique mirror.
And there, on the floor, stood a small white desk and chair.

The small white chair stood perfectly still.
In that chair, writing her letters, sat a pretty little girl.

This girl..... curls and all..... was Gracie.

Chapter 30

Zacky, Bailey, Roley Roanin and Sammy escaped.
They were on Maddy's front porch..... safe and sound.

"That was the most amazing jump ever," said Sammy.
"A snail has never moved so fast and lived to tell about it."

"Going fast is the least of my worries," said Roley Roanin.
"But we were bobbing up and down and all over the place.
  We were flying through the air, completely out of control.
  Zigs and Zags miles up in the air are not my idea of fun."

Bailey shook her head.
"We were only ten or fifteen feet above the ground,
    and I always fly completely in control."

Roley rolled his eyes.
"Fifteen feet to a roley poley feels like miles,
    and I've seen crazy lunatic moths fly straighter.

135

"They are called Luna moths," said Bailey.
"They have much bigger wings than I do.
   Do you want me to ask them to take you for a ride?"

"Absolutely not!" squeaked Roley.
He shivered to think about his flying escape.
   "Next time I'm going to roll my way out of trouble.
   I've been doing that all my life."

Zacky couldn't resist a little teasing.
   "Seems to me," said Zacky,
      "that you are always rolling INTO trouble."

"Very funny," grumbled Roley.

Zacky's smile grew bigger.
   "Were you a little scared?" he asked.
   "It sounds to me like you were a little scared last night."

"I was NOT scared," objected Roley.
"I was just very concerned about the pilot.
   Bailey could have run into a tree branch.
   She needs to be more careful about her flying."

Zacky looked over at Bailey with a teasing smile.
   "Bailey is one of the best flyers in the garden," he said.
   "She is almost as fast as I am."

Roley Roanin quickly defended his butterfly friend.
   "Bailey can fly faster than you any day of the year!
   We beat you here by more than two whole minutes!"

"Well, you and Bailey had a head start!" argued Zacky.

"It seems that only your excuses are super fast," laughed Roley.
"How can you possibly think that you are faster than Bailey?"

"Zacky is super duper fast!" insisted Sammy.
"He saved my life."

"Yeah, I had to carry the snail," said Zacky.

"He's a small snail!" yelled Roley.

"My shell is heavier than it looks," argued Sammy.

Bailey interrupted them.
  "BOYS, BOYS, BOYS! Stop arguing!
   Right now we have more important things to discuss.
   How are we going to stop the Garden Snails?
   Do you have any good ideas?"

  "I have a few ideas," whispered Zacky.
  "But we should go inside to talk.
   You never know if they have spies."

The three friends and their new friend Sammy went inside.
Around Maddy's little wood table, they whispered a plan.
Roley laughed softly and smiled.
It was a very good plan.

Chapter 31

Big Guard decided he would do the right thing.
He left the little guard tied up in the holding chamber,
  and crawled through the tunnels of the old tree stump.
He was going to save the Queen.

Remember when Zacky whispered in Big Guard's ear?
Zacky whispered three things.
The first whisper said:
> "Find the Queen and help her escape.
> Colonel Lampy has her locked away.
> His desire for power has made him dangerous.
> He will risk and ruin everything for power."

Big Guard believed Zacky.
Nobody dangerous should have such power.
So, he went searching for his Queen.
Queen Maggie was in a prison cell, closely guarded.
Big Guard approached the guards on duty.

Big Guard was going to have to trick them.
He put a really mean look on his face,
  and pretended to be in charge.
  "Open up this door and let me in!" he demanded.
  "I have special orders from Colonel Lampy!
    I must deliver a message to the Queen!"

The firefly guards refused.
  "We were given strict orders by the Captain," they said.
  "This door is not to be opened until the Captain returns!"

Big Guard acted tougher and meaner.
  "Well, my orders are more important than your orders!
    My orders come straight from Colonel Lampy himself!"

The firefly guards turned to each other..... worried.
They did not want to get in trouble with Colonel Lampy.
They whispered to each other.

Big Guard waited. He was big. He looked mean.

The firefly guards did not follow the Captain's orders.
One guard opened up a secret panel in the wall.
The other guard took out a key.
They both looked worried.

  "You know we have to shut and lock the door," said a guard.
  "You know..... while you're in there."

  "No problem, little buddy," said Big Guard.
  "Lock me in if you have to. We're all on the same team, right?"

Big Guard patted them on the back.
The firefly guards opened the door.
Big Guard went in to meet the Queen.
The guards pushed on the heavy door to close it,
  but they didn't close it fast.
They listened.

They heard Big Guard make something crash.
Then they heard Big Guard yelling at the Queen.

  "Colonel Lampy is in charge now!" yelled Big Guard.
  "Colonel Lampy will be King of the fireflies!
   He sent me here to MAKE you sign these papers!
   AND SIGN THEM YOU WILL!"

The Firefly guards shut the door all the way and locked it.
They looked at each other and sighed with relief.

  "I'm sure happy we are on Colonel Lampy's side!" said one.

  "With a big mean guard like that," said the other,
    "the Queen doesn't stand a chance!"

Big Guard winked at the Queen as he entered the cell.
The Queen saw him wink and give her a soft smile.
She was sitting in the corner of the small room.
Her chair was a hard, uncomfortable pebble.
There was a little wood table in the room but nothing more.

Big Guard picked up the table and smashed it against the wall.
He yelled at the Queen until the prison door clicked shut.

Then Big Guard whispered to Queen Maggie.
  "I am sorry I have to yell at you, my Queen,
    but I have to make the guards think I'm serious.
  Zacky the Cricket told me you needed help.
  Somehow he knew you were in trouble."

Big Guard started yelling again.
He kicked the broken table around the room.
He smiled and winked at the Queen.

  "I think you should start screaming too," he whispered.
  "And then pretend that I made you fall to the floor."

Queen Maggie nodded to Big Guard.
She screamed with fear in her voice.
  "I will sign the paper!" she cried.
  "I will sign it!
    Just don't hurt me again!"

Big Guard crashed the broken table again.
Then he knocked hard on the door.
  "Open up this door now!" he yelled.
  "NOW!" he yelled again.

The firefly guards rushed to open the prison door.
  "We didn't mean to make you wait."

Queen Maggie was lying on the floor.

  "You better check on the Queen," said Big Guard.
  "I had to get a little tough."

The firefly guards stepped into the prison cell.
They stood over the fallen Queen.
Big Guard quietly turned around,
 and grabbed them both from behind.

Queen Maggie stood up gracefully.
She took the key away from the guards,
 and gave them a regal smile.

 "I am sorry that you choose to serve someone else," she said.
 "Maybe a little time in this room will be good for you.
  You will have plenty of time to think about your choices."

Queen Maggie turned to Big Guard.
 "Thank you for your help."
She dangled the key in the air.
 "Shall we go?" she asked.

The Queen stepped out through the prison cell door.
Big Guard let the firefly guards go.
He stepped backwards out of the room,
 waved goodbye,
 then closed and locked the door.

Respectfully, Big Guard turned to Queen Maggie,
 and told her about the second thing Zacky had whispered.

 "Zacky has gone to talk with the snails," said Big Guard.
 "General Nemoralis is their leader.
  Zacky and his friends are going to surprise him.
  They are meeting at the Old Dirt Patch."

"Then I must leave now to join them," said the Queen calmly. "It is time to repair a broken friendship."

"Sometimes friendships need fixing," smiled Big Guard.

"Big Guard," said the Queen.

"Yes, my Queen."

"The Colonel and his Captain have locked away my friends. Will you help them escape and tell them where I have gone?"

"Yes, my Queen."

"And thank you for everything," she said.

"You're welcome, my Queen."

Queen Maggie gracefully turned.
She walked down the hallway and turned the corner.

Big Guard watched her go.
He knew he had done the right thing.
Now, it was time to help some more.

Zacky had a plan.
This was the last thing Zacky had whispered to him.
He had whispered his plans to Big Guard.
And now Big Guard was going to help.
Big Guard smiled to himself as he walked down the hall.
It was a very good plan.

Chapter 32

General Nemoralis shouted to the Garden Snail troops,
  "Today, we are going to capture the middle garden!
  We have complete control of the lower garden!
  There is no way the garden animals can stop us now!"

Roley Roanin could hear everything the general was saying.
  "I would make a very good spy," he thought to himself.
He watched the Grove snail talking to the army below.

General Nemoralis continued with his speech.
  "WE will attack from all three directions!
  Shiny Shell Soldiers will take the main path.
  Slimy Shell Soldiers will climb the old path.
  Sneaky Shell Soldiers will follow me through the shortcut."

  "We will all meet at the Garden Center.
  When we control the Garden Center, the rest will come easy.
  Does everybody understand these orders?"

"YES, SIR!" answered the snail army troops.
Snail soldiers began to move in all different directions.

Roley Roanin was swinging from a cherry in the cherry tree.
He was hanging upside down and listening to their plans.
And he was more than just spying. He was part of the plan.

"Hey, General!" yelled Roley Roanin.
"I'm up here!"

Roley waved his arms to get the general's attention.
Then he flipped himself right side up.
Now he was standing on top of the cherry,
  swinging back and forth while holding on to the stem.

"Hey, General!" he called out again.
"I'm here to ask you a very important question."

"And what is that?" snarled General Nemoralis.

Roley Roanin smiled a big roley poley smile.
  "Would YOU be willing to surrender?"

"You must be crazy, little bug!" shouted the general.

"I am only supposed to give you one chance!" Roley shouted.
"But, because I am so nice, I will give you a second chance!
  Will you surrender?"

"I WILL NEVER SURRENDER!" shouted the general.

"Would you surrender," Roley paused,
    "if we had you surrounded?"

General Nemoralis responded with confidence.
  "I have you surrounded!" he said.
  "Look below you.
    There will be no escape this time, little bug."

Roley Roanin looked down at the trunk.
Snails surrounded the entire cherry tree.
These snails moved faster than he thought they could.

Roley Roanin looked across the dirt patch.
He looked at Zacky in the old apple tree,
  and waved his arms back and forth.
  "Hey, Zacky!" shouted Roley Roanin.
  "The General has me surrounded!"

General Nemoralis followed Roley's eyes.
He, too, looked up into the old apple tree.

Resting comfortably against the stem of a green apple,
  Zacky looked down at the army of Garden Snails.
  "Hello, General," he said.
  "I'd offer you and your friends an apple,
      but they aren't quite ripe yet.
    Apples that are not ripe can give you a tummy ache.
    And you don't want that on your long trip home.
    You and your friends are looking very lost.
    Can we help you with some directions?"

"We are not lost, little cricket," said General Nemoralis.
"We have no intention of leaving this beautiful garden."

"Then why are you destroying it?" asked Bailey.

General Nemoralis turned around.
He followed the sweet sound of Bailey's butterfly voice.

"Why are you destroying it?" she asked again.

Bailey settled down onto the branch of a wilting butterfly bush.
This bush was already sick because of the snails.

General Nemoralis did not answer her.
He looked back at Roley Roanin,
   then turned to look at Zacky.

"Well, the three of you definitely have me surrounded!
   Are there any more?" asked General Nemoralis sarcastically.

At that very moment a Garden Snail soldier yelled out,
   "Look up there, on Mulch Hill."

Zacky, Roley and Bailey searched the hillside.
General Nemoralis and his snail troops searched too.
At first, there was nothing much to see.
Above Mulch Hill hovered a small group of fireflies.
Then, lines of small wormy soldiers appeared.
Hundreds of them lined up across the top.

The glowworm army had arrived.

Chapter 33

Firefly Colonel Lampy flew over Mulch Hill.
He was very proud of his glowworm army.
Forty of his special firefly guards followed him.
The Colonel searched for the Firefly Captain,
 and found him.

"The troops look excellent," said Colonel Lampy.

"Thank you, SIR!" answered the Captain.

"Hold them here until I return," commanded the Colonel.

"Yes, SIR!"

Colonel Lampy flew up and away from his glowworm army.
Forty firefly guards followed him faithfully.
Colonel Lampy confided in them.
They listened to his plans.

"I will observe this snail army for myself," said Lampy.
"I will let them see the full force of my army.
  I will offer their leader one chance to surrender.
  Maybe they will surrender without a fight.
  If they refuse to surrender, I will crush them."

With his loyal guards surrounding him,
  Colonel Lampy flew toward the Old Dirt Patch.
He would make this army of Garden Snails surrender,
  and then he would control them.
With the power of the Glowworm and Garden Snail armies,
  Colonel Lampy could control all of Gracie's Garden.
Then, he would be more than just the King of the Fireflies!
He would become King of Gracie's Garden.

Colonel Lampy dreamed of power.
He would risk everything to have it.

Chapter 34

Zacky leaned casually against the apple's stem.
General Nemoralis turned and looked up at him.
  "I see that you have reinforcements, little cricket.
    This will definitely make the fight more interesting."

  "General," said Zacky, "those are not our soldiers."

  "Nope, those are not our soldiers!" yelled Roley.
  "But this sure is going to be one heck of a fight!
    There must be over a thousand glowworms up on Mulch Hill.
    And that's only what I can see from here!"

Bailey could not keep quiet.
  "No one should be talking about fighting!
    We should be talking about how to solve our problems."

  "Bailey is right," Zacky called out to Roley.
  "We should be trying to solve our problems with words."

Zacky looked over toward Mulch Hill.
  "But by seeing this large and powerful glowworm army,
    maybe General Nemoralis will reconsider his plans.
   Moving into the middle garden will not be easy.
   The glowworms will fight hard to protect their homes.
   Maybe there is a way to solve our problems without fighting."
Zacky looked to the general; "Wouldn't you agree?"

General Nemoralis stood silent and the snail army stood still.
None of the Garden Snail troops were moving.
They saw the glowworm army up on Mulch Hill,
  and waited for their general to give them orders.

General Nemoralis looked up at the glowworm army.
  "This army of glowworms changes nothing," said the general.
  "I have come here to conquer Gracie's Garden,
    and that is what I am going to do!"

  "GARDEN SNAIL TROOPS!" bellowed General Nemoralis.
  "GET READY TO FIGHT!"

The Garden Snails clinked their shells.
They moved slowly toward Mulch Hill.
Some of them were loud and excited.
Some of them were quiet and calm.
All of them were scared.

  "Hey, Zacky," yelled Roley Roanin.
  "I see a group of those flying lightbulbs coming our way."

Zacky could see them too. Colonel Lampy was almost there.

Chapter 35

Colonel Lampy and his forty firefly guards flew.
As they circled the dirt patch and the Garden Snail army,
  he called out orders to his guards:
        "Form a circle in the air above me!
          Watch for any signs of danger!
          Be ready to fly!"

Then Colonel Lampy hovered down.
  "I am Colonel Lampy!" he announced.
  "I am the commander of the glowworm army.
    Who is the leader of this army of snails?"

"NOT ME!" yelled Roley Roanin, "NOT ME!"

Up in the cherry tree, Roley waved his arms and legs.
He caught all of Colonel Lampy's attention.
Roley Roanin smiled big, rolled his eyes,
  and pointed at General Nemoralis.

153

"It's HIM," shouted Roley.
"His name is General Nemoralis,
  and he's bigger and meaner than you."

Colonel Lampy turned around to ignore the little roley poley.
All puffed up with authority, he shouted down to the snails,
    "I am here to demand your surrender!
    Surrender to me! King of the Fireflies!"

"You are not King of the Fireflies," said Zacky.
"Queen Maggie is your ruler!"

"Mind your own business, little jumping bug!"
Colonel Lampy said it very rudely.

General Nemoralis spoke out for everyone to hear.
  "It does not matter who you are, little lightning bug.
  I have no intentions of surrendering to anyone."

"Hey, Colonel Lamp-Head!" yelled Roley Roanin.
"I could have told you that.
  I already asked the General to surrender.
  I even asked him twice!"

"Bugs and snails!" Bailey's sweet, loving voice called out.
"Why does anyone need to fight?
  There is plenty of work to be done in the world!"

Everyone looked at Bailey.
And for a moment, they were silent.
They knew Bailey was right.

But then, Colonel Lampy spoke.

He talked softly at first.
"I cannot allow these snails to destroy our garden.
So, I must fight to destroy them.
Besides, these snails will make an excellent meal.
They will help me to grow my glowworm army."

Then Colonel Lampy talked louder.
"I will have more glowworms.
I will have more lightning bugs.
I will take complete control of Gracie's Garden.
Every little flying, jumping, crawling and rolling bug
will have to listen to me!"

Finally, he was shouting.
"I Am Now The KING of The FIREFLIES!
And I Will BECOME,
The KING of GRACIE'S GARDEN!"

There was silence, but only for a moment.
The silence was interrupted by a beautiful voice.

"Colonel Lampy, you will never be King of anything."

Everyone looked up to see her.
The Garden Snails stood still.
Bailey smiled with fluttering wings.

Colonel Lampy sneered.
He was not happy that she was there.

General Nemoralis was impressed.
She was absolutely stunning.

Zacky gave a deep bow and sang a low musical note.
This musical note lasted longer than usual.
And at the end of the note, he chirped.

Roley Roanin? He had never seen her before.
He could not believe how beautiful a bug could be.
His eyes twirled and his mouth hung open.
Roley Roanin was speechless as he stumbled backwards,
  and almost fell out of the cherry tree.

Queen Maggie had arrived.

Chapter 36

Big Guard yelled, "One! Two! Three! PUSSHHH!"
Big Guard yelled again, "One! Two! Three! PUSSHHH!"
There was a quiet creaking sound.

Big Guard had one hundred firefly guards helping him.
They were all loyal to the Queen.

 "AGAIN!" yelled Big Guard.
 "One! Two! Three! PUSSHHH!
  One! Two! Three! PUSSHHH!"

The handle turned. It creaked open.
Water flowed through the big green tube.
Big Guard listened to the power of the water.
With all their strength, the lightning bugs pushed.
Again and again and again, the handle turned.

This was Zacky's plan, the last important whisper to Big Guard.

Big Guard flew up into the air.
They were following Zacky's instructions perfectly.
He watched the royal guards turn the handle.

"Keep pushing," Big Guard called out.
"I'm going to check the wheelbarrow."

Big Guard flew off.
A few of the guards flew with him.
Off to the Garden Center, they went.
They went to check their work.
Their work was already working.

The little blue wheelbarrow was wet.
Cold clear water rushed out of the long green tube.
Overflowing the top of Gracie's pink watering can,
  water splashed down onto her garden tools.
The wheelbarrow was filling up quickly.

"Zacky was right!" said Big Guard.

Big Guard watched the water level rise.
The watering can and tools were all on one side.
The wheelbarrow was completely out of balance.

Big Guard smiled.
  "I just hope Zacky and his friends have enough time."

As the water climbed higher, the wheelbarrow started to tilt.
Yes, the wheelbarrow started to tilt!

Chapter 37

Maddy ran across the floor of Gracie's room.
Buster Bumbler followed her.
Maddy looked up.

Gracie's white chair was decorated.
Pretty ribbons and colorful strings climbed up,
 and all around it.

Maddy whispered to Bumbler,
 "I think it would be best if you wait here.
 Keep still..... here under the chair.
 Sometimes little girls can be afraid of bumble bees."

"I'll be waiting for your signal," said Bumbler.

Maddy climbed up the pretty ribbons and colorful strings
 that hung from Gracie's chair.

With her little hand, she tapped Gracie on the shoulder.
Gracie turned her head and smiled with surprise.

"Oh, my little Maddy!" she exclaimed.
Gracie held out her hand. Maddy crawled in.
Maddy sat sweetly in Gracie's palm,
 feeling very safe.

Questions just bubbled out of Gracie.
She asked one question after another,
 and didn't stop to wait for the answers.

"What are you doing out of the garden?
Are you here all by yourself?
How did you get here?
Did someone leave the garden gate open again?
Are Zacky, Bailey and Roley Roanin alright?
Do you know how dangerous this is?
Are you alright?"

Maddy waved her hands at Gracie.
She wanted Gracie to calm down.

Then she waved to Buster Bumbler.
She wanted Bumbler to fly up and join her.

Gracie calmed down and Bumbler flew up.
He carefully and slowly settled down on Gracie's desk.

"Is this handsome bumble bee your friend?" asked Gracie.

Maddy nodded, "Yes."

Gracie held her hand out again.
She was not afraid of a bumble bee.
Bumbler walked slowly over Gracie's fingers to Maddy.

Maddy waved for Gracie to bring them closer.
Gracie raised them both up in the palm of her hand.
Then Gracie asked them softly and sweetly,

    "Will you please tell me what is going on?"

The two friends talked about what was happening in the garden.
They told Gracie everything.

Chapter 38

"Time for me to go," said Sammy out loud to himself.
He heard Zacky's special musical note, followed by a chirp.
That musical note followed by a chirp was a secret code.
It was the signal for which Sammy was waiting.

Sammy slid out from behind Crystal Ledge.
This large rock was filled with sparkling gems.
It was a piece of Gracie's crystal stone chair.
Freezing water in winter had cracked it away,
  and Gracie had placed it above the short-cut drainpipe.
Crystal Ledge looked out over the Old Dirt Patch.

Sammy slid out slowly.
It was time for him to be part of a plan.
He pulled himself over the top of the crystal stone,
  and slid to the edge of Crystal Ledge.
Shiny, sparkling gemstones surrounded Sammy.
From up there, Sammy could see everyone!

Bailey..... on the wilting butterfly bush.
Zacky..... up in the apple tree.
Roley..... swinging in the cherry tree.
General Nemoralis..... in the dirt patch below.
The Snail Army..... facing toward Mulch Hill.
The Glowworm Army..... on top of Mulch Hill.
Colonel Lampy..... in the air with his loyal guards.
And Queen Maggie..... in the air with her royal guards.

Sammy stood by himself on Crystal Ledge.
Suddenly, a single ray of sunlight struck the crystal.
Light blazed across the crystal stone,
　and all the sparkling gems reflected.

Rays of brilliant light exploded.
All different colors went all different directions,
　except where Sammy stood.
Brilliant white light surrounded him.

Sammy the Snail was glowing.
He looked larger than life.
He took a deep breath into his lungs and yelled.
Sammy yelled for the first time in his life.

"HELLOOO!!!"

Everyone looked up at Sammy on Crystal Ledge.
Colonel Lampy forgot about Queen Maggie.
Queen Maggie forgot about Colonel Lampy.
It was the most amazing sight the four friends had ever seen.
It was the scariest site the Garden Snails had ever seen.

"IT'S a DECOLLATE SNAIL!" yelled General Nemoralis.

Snail army officers yelled out loudly,
  "ALL Snail Troops! Protect the General!"

Some of the Garden Snails went crazy with fear.
  "Protect your babies!" they cried.
  "There's a Decollate snail!"

The Garden Snail army turned away from Mulch Hill.
They moved quickly to surround General Nemoralis,
  then looked up to Crystal Ledge.
The soldiers stared at Sammy, silently afraid.

There is one fact that all Garden Snails know.
Decollate snails are dangerous.

Chapter 39

"Hello," said Sammy waving to the crowd below.
"I would like to introduce myself to everyone.
   I am Sammy the Snail."

All the Garden Snails gasped. The rumors were true.
A real live Decollate snail was living in Gracie's Garden,
   and he was standing right in front of them.

The snail army could not believe their eyes.
Decollate snails are in scary snail picture books.
Decollate snails are the monsters in scary bedtime stories.
Decollate snails are the creatures in terrifying nightmares.
Decollate snails are dangerous.
Because they eat little Garden Snails and Garden Snail eggs!

The Garden Snails shuddered as they moved closer together.
Not one had ever met a real Decollate snail before.

For the first time, General Nemoralis looked concerned.

Sammy straightened up and spoke again.
  "I would like to say Welcome!"

The Garden Snails looked at each other.
This Decollate snail sounded gentle and kind.
And he didn't look that scary.

Sammy continued with his speech.
  "I have only met a few Garden Snails in my life.
   They were afraid of me and ran away.
   No other snails would spend time with me.
   I have been so lonely here in Gracie's Garden.
   I have been..... all by myself."

  "I planned to leave Gracie's Garden forever.
   I was convinced that this garden was not my home.
   But others have shown me; a home is where you make it.
   These others have become my very best friends.
   I would like to thank them from the insides of my shell."

Sammy took a bow,
  then straightened up and pointed at Bailey.

He spoke to the crowds below.
  "Bailey the Butterfly welcomed me to Gracie's Garden.
   Her gentle laugh and sweet smile comfort me.
   Whenever I am with her, I feel important..... and at ease.
   She is always sweet and kind and caring and loving.
   Can we all give her a big round of applause?"

168

Sammy the Snail clicked his shell softly.
Roley Roanin whistled and cheered.
Zacky chirped with musical notes.
Queen Maggie glowed like a queen.

Very few of the Garden Snails clicked.
All of them watched Sammy closely.
They were nervous about being so close to him.

Sammy pointed to Roley Roanin.
  "Roley Roanin welcomed me with a smile.
   He gave me a place to stay in his home.
   Others would have thrown me out.
   He put his good-natured trust in me.
   Can we all give Roley Roanin a round of applause?"

Sammy the snail clicked his shell softly.
Bailey fluttered her wings.
Zacky chirped with musical notes.
Queen Maggie glowed like a queen.

And Roley Roanin?
He took big deep bows Over and Over and Over again.
He pushed and pulled the Garden Snails with his postive energy.
Some of the snails laughed and many of them clicked loudly.

  "Thank you! Thank you! Thank you!" yelled Roley.
He waved his hands vigorously at the snail army.
Now, most of the snails were smiling and clicking.
Roley Roanin bowed again.
He just loved all the attention.

Sammy cleared his throat.
Roley Roanin calmed the crowd of snails.

Sammy continued,
  "Next, I would like to thank a friend of mine who is not here.
   Maddy M. Mouse took me in and gave me shelter.
   When I was hungry, she gave me food to eat.
   When I was thirsty, she gave me something cool to drink.
   Can we all give Maddy a big round of applause?"

All the snails were clicking now.
Roley Roanin yelled and screamed.
He clapped, whistled and stomped all his feet.
The snails clicked louder and louder.
Roley Roanin's energy moved the crowd.
Zacky and Queen Maggie smiled and watched the show.
Bailey giggled at the super-silly roley poley.
Colonel Lampy and General Nemoralis frowned.

  "AND Finally!" Sammy yelled, trying to get their attention.
  "And Finally, I would like to thank Zacky the Cricket!
   When I was lost, he looked for me..... found me,
      and set me free. Zacky saved me.
   Let's all give Zacky a round of applause!"

This time the crowd went wild.
They were clicking and clapping and cheering and whistling.
Roley Roanin? Break-dancing in the cherry tree!
He was working the crowd of snails into a fit.
Zacky and Queen Maggie laughed out loud.
The colonel and the general did not.

"Excuse me! Excuse me!" Sammy cleared his throat.
"Excuse ME!" Sammy called out louder.

Finally, the crowd settled down.

"There is one more thing I need to tell you," said Sammy.
"There is one more....."

From up above, a buzzing sound interrupted him.
Now remember, buzzing sounds in the garden can be good,
   or..... buzzing sounds in the garden can be bad.
The friends and the crowd went silent.

Like an Air-Force jet, Buster Bumbler rumbled overhead.
He buzzed right over Sammy's head.
And then, he buzzed over the crowd of snails.

Roley Roanin recognized him right away.
He yelled and cheered.

  "BUM---BLER!   BUM---BLER!   BUM---BLER!"

The crowd below followed Roley Roanin enthusiastically.
They all clicked and cheered and yelled,
  "BUM--- BLER!   BUM---BLER!"

Sammy tried to interrupt them.
He tried to warn them.
This crowd was out of control!
     Laughing and Cheering!
Clicking and Clapping and Stomping!

Sammy tried again.
  "EXCUSE ME! EXCUSE ME!"

Sammy tried to warn them.
But it was too late.

Chapter 40

The ground shook.
The crowd went silent.
Everybody stopped and stood still.
And then..... it happened.

The top of Mulch Hill went missing.
The entire glowworm army disappeared.
A tidal wave of water washed them all away.

The army of snails could not believe their eyes.

Colonel Lampy gasped and flew away.
All of his hard work and planning..... gone.
His entire army of glowworms..... missing.
A few seconds of time had taken away
  every dream that Colonel Lampy could dream.

General Nemoralis cheered.

"I will have Victory!!!" cheered the General.
"NOBODY can stop me now!"

General Nemoralis looked up at Zacky in the old apple tree.
  "The snail gods are with me!" he yelled.
  "ME! ME! ME!"

The army of snails did not cheer with General Nemoralis.
What happened to the glowworm army wasn't fair.

A few seconds passed.
Everyone thought it was over.
But then, Crystal Ledge began to shake violently.
The ground around Crystal Ledge rumbled.
Sammy used his special snail slime.
He stuck himself to the hard stone crystal floor.

The water rushed.
It rushed over Crystal Ledge and through the drainpipe.
Sammy disappeared in a waterfall from above.
Garden Snails were swallowed up by water that rushed below.
The massive flood of water created a whirlpool.
The crowd of snails could not hold themselves to the dirt.
A thousand Garden Snails swirled around in chaos,
  and then all of them were washed away.

Well, almost all of them.

From the heavens above,
  a little girl's hand grabbed General Nemoralis from the flood.

Chapter 41

Gracie smiled.

She beamed with joy.

She held a very pretty Grove snail in her hand.

"You are the most beautiful snail I have ever seen.
   I am going to make a special place for you in my garden.
   Gracie's Garden will be your special home forever."

Gracie showed Maddy the fancy looking Grove snail.
   "Oh, Maddy, isn't he beautiful?"

Maddy watched everything.

She snuggled in Gracie's pretty pocket.

This pocket was sewn in the center of Gracie's sundress,
   resting just below Gracie's heart.

"Oh, look, Maddy!" giggled Gracie.

"I found our little Sammy too."

Gracie reached down onto Crystal Ledge for Sammy.
She picked him up and placed him gently in her hand,
  the same hand that held General Nemoralis.
Sammy smiled at him.

General Nemoralis looked scared and tried to move away.
Sammy just smiled.

Gracie picked up General Nemoralis and moved him back.
  "Now you two are going to have to get along.
    There is plenty of room in my garden for the both of you!"

Buster Bumbler and Queen Maggie flew over to Maddy.
They landed on the ruffles of Gracie's sundress.

Zacky jumped from the old apple tree onto Gracie's shoulder.
Bailey did two loops in the air,
  and landed on the very same shoulder,
  right next to Zacky.
Zacky beat her by a millisecond.

Maddy looked up at them from the pocket of Gracie's sundress.
  "Well, Bailey, it looks like Zacky has beaten you this time."

Zacky and Bailey looked at each other.
      "It was a tie!"
They both said it at the same time,
  and all three friends laughed.

Gracie was happy to have so many friends close by.
She smiled at Sammy and held him close.

With love and affection, she spoke to him.
  "Sammy, you are very important to me and my garden.
    I am going to build a very special house just for you."

  "My Daddy says soon you will have a family of your own.
    He says it only takes one Decollate snail to start a family.
    So, I hope you will decide to stay in my garden.
    I want you to make it your home forever."

Sammy felt all warm inside.
He started to blush,
  but the warm tender moment was shattered.

    "WATCH OUT BELOWWWWWWWWWW!"

The amazing Roley Roanin jumped out of the cherry tree.
He fell with a triple twist into the palm of Gracie's hand.
He rolled around both snails several times,
  somersaulted into the air and landed on his feet.
He landed right next to General Nemoralis.

Roley Roanin put his arm around the General's shoulder.
He smiled his biggest Roley Roanin smile ever,
  while pulling General Nemoralis close to him.
Roley looked him straight in the eye and whispered loudly.

    "You Got Me!"

Chapter 42

Sammy ended his short speech.
  "This has been the most exciting day of my life.
  Thank you, friends, for being my friends.
  And thank you all for having this great party!"

With his mouth filled full of cocoa brownies and blackberry pie,
  Roley Roanin yelled, "No --oblem -t all!"

The other guests laughed.
  "What did he say?" they asked.

Zacky hopped closer to Roley Roanin,
With his arm around Roley's shoulder, he spoke out to the crowd.
  "That's secret code for..... NO PROBLEM AT ALL!"

The crowd of guests laughed even louder.
Zacky and Roley raised their acorn caps.
Sweet lemonade splashed over the rims.

"We want to make a toast!" they said together.
Roley Roanin's mouth was still full of food,
  so Zacky did most of the talking.

  "First..... A Toast to Maddy!
  Thank you for risking your life to save Gracie's Garden.
  Thank you for having this party for all of our friends.
  HIP HIP HOORAY!"

Everybody raised their acorn caps and cheered.
They clapped and clicked and stomped and whistled.

Zacky and Roley yelled over the noise of the crowd.
  "Second..... A Toast to Bailey!
  Thank you for all your hard work.
  Your work makes this garden continue to grow.
  The garden brings us all this wonderful food and drink.
  HIP HIP HOORAY!"

The crowd cheered even louder.

  "Third..... A Toast to all our friends and neighbors!
  We thank General Buster Bumbler for protecting Maddy.
  We thank Big Guard for helping to free Queen Maggie.
  We thank Queen Maggie for starting new friendships.
  And thanks to all those special bugs,
    working to make Gracie's Garden a better place to live."

Everyone at the party gave them a thundering applause.
Whistling and cheering filled Maddy's little country home.
Zacky and Roley calmed the crowd down.

It wasn't easy. Everyone was having such a good time.
Roley Roanin finally swallowed the last of his food,
  and Zacky hushed the crowd.
For a moment, there was silence.

Zacky and Roley stood up straight and tall.
Then they spoke together with all sincerity.

"And finally!
        Most of all!
                We want to thank Gracie!

  Without Gracie..... there would not be..... a Gracie's Garden."

Everyone at the party cheered.
The eating and drinking and talking and laughing continued.
The celebration lasted all through the night.

The only one to go to sleep that night
        was a little girl with a head full of curls.
                And her name,

Gracie

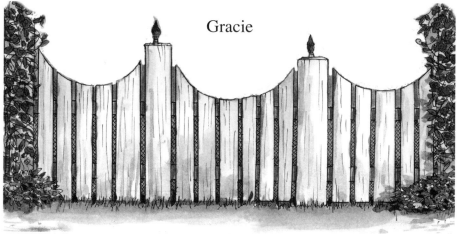

Gracie's Garden II -Compost Cliffs- Coming Spring 2011!

Chapter 2

Sammy and his three girls sat on Crystal Ledge. This is where they liked to watch the sunrise. That's right! Sammy has a little snail family of his own just like Gracie's dad said he would. Remember, you only need one snail to make a family.

Sammy enjoyed these first few hours of morning. Sunlight bounced around on Crystal Ledge. All the gems were twinkling again!

"Oh, look at the colors!" said the littlest one.
"They're beautiful!" said Matilda.
"I love to watch the sun rise," said the eldest one.

Sammy looked out over the Old Dirt Patch. Golden sunlight washed over Gracie's Garden. He thought about his little house. He thought about his three little girls. He thought about his friends. This was Sammy's home. Sammy looked back to the girls and finished the last line of his story.

"And right there," he pointed to the Old Dirt Patch below, "the Great Garden Snail Army was washed away."

" Papa, did all the Garden Snails die?" asked the girls.

Sammy laughed as he told them again,

"No, my little girls. They did not."

"What happened to them?" they asked.

These girls already knew the ending of Sammy's story. They had listened to his story a dozen times. But the girls enjoyed listening to it over and over and over again. They never grew tired of hearing it.

"Please tell us," asked the littlest one.
"Please tell us."

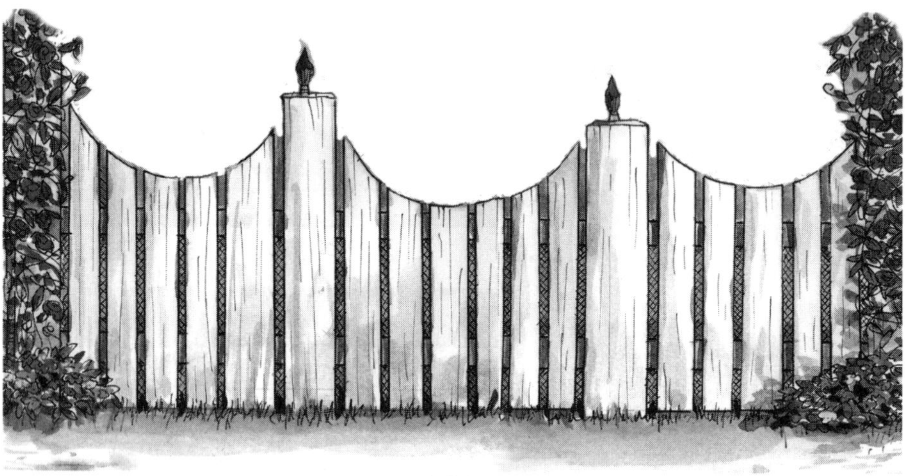

I want to thank you for reading
Gracie's Garden.

Please visit us at:
graciesgardenthebook.com

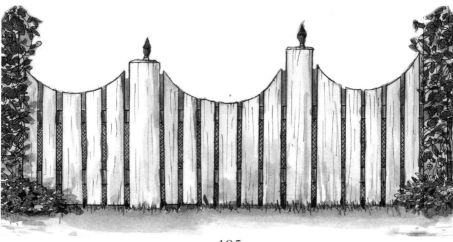

Special thanks to:

Bruce Collier
Ann Hogan
Ronda Birtha

eimaj publishing is a small press publishing company.